DEDICATED TO THOSE
WHO WILL NEVER READ
WHAT THEY INSPIRED.

Matador
9 Priory Business Park,
Wistow Road, Kibworth Beauchamp,
Leicestershire. LE8 0RX
Tel: 0116 279 2299
Email: books@troubador.co.uk
Web: www.troubador.co.uk/matador
Twitter: @matadorbooks

ISBN 978 1785892 721

British Library Cataloguing in Publication Data.
A catalogue record for this book is available from the British Library.

Printed and bound by CPI Group (UK) Ltd, Croydon, CR0 4YY

Matador is an imprint of Troubador Publishing Ltd

If you are reading this I am dead.

Or alive.

Either/or.

Or possibly neither.

My name is Codename Alexander McCuba: explorer, bladesman and Guildsman of the Guild of Adventurers.

This is not, however, my real name. My real name is a secret, hidden somewhere about my person in case I forget it.

This is my Ninth Great Adventure.

It is not going to plan.

What started out as a simple rum run has gone…awry. To put it mildly.

I scribble these words in Parts Unknown, using a piece of driftwood and a small vial of ink that I keep hidden in my beard for emergencies.

For this is an emergency!

I have lost my Book of Deeds – along with everything I don't keep on my person at all times. All records of my feats and achievements are gone. I am Deedless: a man without a story. A fate worse than death, some would say.

I enscribble this, therefore, partly to log what could be my final days, and partly as a record of who I am and the Guild I represent.

MY OTHER 8 ADVENTURES

1. Hunted, chased and challenged the behemoth penguin Shivering Rodriguez, then defeated him in single combat with a single flying knee (to the knee). This is why I am also known as "He of the Knee."

2. Survived Ingangaga (→ Inganga?), deepest and most lethal of shamanic trances, without crying out for soothing balms. Thus I earned my beard.

3. Completed the year-long Great Ham Race, across land, sea, sky and the bizarre inflatable world of Phloom, where I was temporarily jellified. My fellow racers now know me as "Ol' Jellyface." (aka Wobbles)

4. Battled the maddening Shrubus Infernalalis and smashed its leaves to create Punch Spice, the active ingredient in Medicinal Rum – the only known cure for chronic sobriety. This earned me my place as an apprentice in the Guild Apothecary.

5. Scaled the deceptively innocuous-sounding Cake Mountain during the terrible storm o' crows, and planted the flag Vinflik at the summit to claim it for the Guild. The flag later sank into the frosting, or so I am told.

6. Freed the ancient camel Saul the Dashing from harsh captivity on the Tal-Tol border, and rode him back to safety in Quaalpath via a daring crossing of the thrice-frozen planes of Dün-Né. Hence my title, Camelfriend.

7. Spent nine days and nights hunched over a tiny anvil, forging Gullgronrak – the famous Golden Beard Brush – as a prize for the Guild Games. It was later stolen. By me. This I must confess, lest it haunt me in these final days.

8. Lasted an entire Clan Harris feast, including the notorious Steak Race Challenge, a full-blown pudding dance, and a 3-day long rendition of the drinking game "Drinking with Steve". I took no title for performing this deed, but I am now an official member of the extended Harris family. Truly, this is more trouble than it is worth.

SS-1

LOG ENTRY: ONE
The Quest So far → A RUM RUN

By the Nine Big Faces, where to begin?

I was sent on a quest. That much is for sure. My task was to pick up our latest shipment of rum, and my instructions were simple:

Thus I departed.

With hindsight, I realise I should have asked somebody *what*, *or who*, *or where* the **Great Extravaganza** is.

That was an oversight on my part.

I see that now.

But I was so EXCITED!

To be sent on a solo quest – by the Guildmaster himself – is a ~~huge~~ honour. HUGE!

When such an opportunity is thrown your way, you do not stop to ask questions.

You leap – boots first – into an adventure!

So I leapt (onto a ship, as it happened) and set out in search of the Great Extravaganza.

I have some theories as to what a great extravaganza could be:

THE GREAT EXTRAVAGANZA COULD BE:

- A never-ending feast, which I must infiltrate by disguising myself as some kind of exotic princess.
- A vast rumpository on the top of a mountain, which I must climb blindfolded and unaided – perhaps with neither food nor water.
- A monstrous beast guarding its long-accumulated rum stash, which I must battle bare-fisted and bellowing.
- A mysterious travelling circus, which I must join by developing a curious variety of useless skills.
- A metaphor for my own personal development, which I will discover at an opportune moment in the not-too-distant future.

My search took me far and wide, from Buridan's Shrine to the Singing Mountains of El Hanan, until even the ocean itself became far from recognisable.

In fact, it became downright abusive. I first noticed things were taking a turn for the strange when I strolled from my cabin one morning (after a particularly mighty breakfeast) and noticed the sea had turned a curious shade of mauve. (Some might call it magenta, but I would duel them with blunted axes to prove otherwise).

I observed the ocean for some time, sketching the patterns of the waves and noting its habits. Alas, I suppose all those meticulous records are now lost forever. As the days wore on, I sensed the sea was becoming increasingly (for lack of a better word) malicious: tossing my ship around when I was practising the Nine Great Poses; splashing the deck whenever I made a cheery fire; calling me names behind my back...

At first I thought the isolation was simply driving me delusional (again), but then I distinctively heard a wave call me a 'pompous git' as it floated by. Enraged, I hurled my whaling-spear into the water. It had little impact. The wave simply jeered at my efforts and floated on by. My harpoon had been lampooned.

Furious, I bunched my mighty quadriceps to leap overboard.

I intend to punch the wave right in the swell. Then suddenly (perhaps sensing the danger) the sea snatched up my ship like the penultimate vol-au-vent in an otherwise tedious assortment of canapés, and dashed it against the rocks!

When I regained consciousness, I was... ashore.

I cleared the dirt from my beard and took a look around. All was darkness, as if a gritty black curtain had been drawn across the land. I paused to clear the dirt from my eyes, and took another look around. It was much more productive.

I was on a beach:

A vast expanse of golden yellow that, upon closer inspection, turned out to be made of tiny grains of sand - not gold.

(This was a shame; I love the taste of gold in the morning and it has been a while since any of my adventures have proved profitable in the monetary sense.)

All that remained of my boat was some driftwood and a smattering of my possessions, which had been washed ashore. The rest, including my log books, collection of throwing hammers and personal Book of Deeds (which every Guildsman must carry) are presumably at the bottom of the ocean.

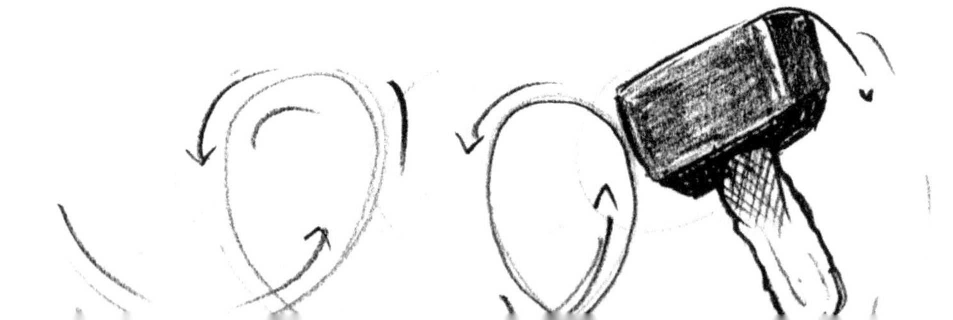

REMAINING EQUIPMENT AND ABILITIES

- **THIS ONE REMAINING LOG BOOK:** *all my quests hitherto have been lost.*

* **ADVENTURING BOOTS:** both invincible and fashionable.

o **FEASTING ROBES:** somewhat tattered and soggy, but undeniably majestic.

✓ **DIGNITY:** remains intact, if somewhat nebulous.

→ **PRESTIGIOUS STRENGTH OF ARM:** I tested this by hurling a rock. It has yet to descend.

"What goes up must continue to go up."

(Forever, if one is to pass the Guild's Test of Strength.)

* **Sense of humour:** a blind man strolls into a tavern. I offer him some mead. Joke complete. (Mead makes people do funny things and, because this man is blind, he'll probably do something even funnier on account of all the objects into which he could unknowingly bump. He could spill a drink, for example, or attempt to dance with a horse. I shan't go on; the humorous implications of this situation are numerous and I am a busy man.)

× **RUMPASS:** is attached to me permanently.

+ **META-HAT:** found dangling around my neck by its cord.

▲ **GUILDSMAN'S HANDBOOK:** waterproof, fireproof, critic-proof and, apparently, miraculously buoyant.

Behind me was a range of jagged mountains, all topped with snow despite the blazing sun which, when I glanced at it to tell the time, winked and waved at me with gloved hands.

This was a little concerning, so I distracted myself in an attempt to count all the sand on the beach. *If I could count the number of grains of sand in a single handful, I could simply multiply that by the number of handfuls on the beach to discover roughly how many grains there were in total.*

I counted up to **13,252** before I realised the futility of my task. I made a gentleman's estimation of exactly five billion and returned to my studies of the land. It was then that I spied a hairy-looking fellow on the beach, clad in a floral shirt and sipping a cocktail. I took heart; as we say in the Guild:

"Where drink ~~abounds,~~ hope" ~~flows free.~~"

DRINK = HOPE

I approached the stranger and greeted him in the customary Guildsman's manner - with a list of my deeds and titles. I then moved swiftly into the Nine Great Poses; the Great Greeting Dance of the Guild, which shows that we mean no harm - and are capable of summoning a startling turn of agility when necessary.

It was then that I realised this man was far larger and far, far hairier than I had fist realised. And I scribble these words as a famously large and infamously hairy man myself.

FAR!

Before I could gird my loins, he extended a large hand - clad in a curious white glove - and introduced himself.

4?

"Yeti" he is called.

LOG ENTRY: TWO
Yeti and The Sauce

I am spending my time with Yeti, learning about this land and observing life on the beach. Whether Yeti speaks my tongue or my Guildsence allows me to understand and speak his language without even realising, I do not know.

The beach is a busy place, bustling with people of all manner of different 'races', but none that I recognise. Most of them are humanish if not humanoid. Like Yeti, for example; although he seems to be a one off.

Thus far, this place has been unlike any other I have stumbled upon before. I am also stumbling more than usual, but I put this down to my inexperience in walking around on sand in sturdy adventuring boots.

Yeti is a delightful fellow, if slightly odd. He sings to his axe, for example. He claims to be 'enchanting' it, but I think he should lay off whatever he packs into his pipe. He spends most his time humming to himself and using his axe to carve large leaf-shaped boards out of a dwindling stockpile of 'enchanted wood'.

He tells me he cuts the wood from Vewdu Trees on the other side of the island, called the Thundra. Apparently it takes on some very curious properties if you harvest it beneath the light of the full moon.

This is no surprise. We Guildsman are very familiar with the powers of the full moon. Our own strength, for example, doubles when the moon is at its fullest.

As luck would have it, we possess a limitless supply of potent drink, which is lubricating our intercourse.

Wait.

Let me rephrase that.

We have a limitless supply of potent drink, which is...alleviating the social tension and instigating light-hearted conversation. Much better. I don't want to give the wrong impression; I like Yeti, but he's not my type. Although he does bear a striking resemblance to my fourth wife...

Let's move swiftly on, shall we?

We fetch our drinks from a nearby river: a free-flowing stream of intoxicating bliss, upon which I stumbled (*to my shock, excitement and subsequent regret*) the first time I went for a swim.

I am unsure of the exact content of the river, but Yeti tells me it flows from some mysterious place high in the mountains, called "The Sauce".

Many explorers have set out to find The Sauce, yet **none** have **ever succeeded**. It's the hangovers that get them, apparently. Especially at altitude.

This sounds an awful lot like a challenge to me.

Confusingly, the islanders also refer to the liquid itself as "sauce". At least, I think that's confusing. Perhaps it makes total sense.

The sauce is clouding my judgment. I think.

LOG ENTRY: THREE
The Rumpass

To be honest, I am appreciating this unexpected break from my quest.

I don't often enjoy sitting still; we Guildsmen are cursed with a furious energy that must have an outlet, lest it turn upon itself like a serpent biting its own tail, or fist...punching itself...forever...

Yet the destruction of my ship has forced me to take some time out and appreciate my need to relax. This island seems the ideal place to do so. Soon enough, I shall build a new ship and be on my way.

Yeti is curious to find out more about me and where I come from. He cannot understand my lack of gloves, for example. I told him a Guildsman only wears gloves when at risk of frostbite, or engaging in the noble sport of Punch Face.

He still cannot get his head around it. I shall bear this in mind if we ever play Punch Face. It is a sport in which getting your head around things makes up at least half the challenge.

I asked Yeti whether he ever takes his gloves off.
He just laughed. I shan't press the matter.

OTHER THINGS AFFECTED BY THE FULL MOON

Beard growth: increases by 0.3 times

Shoes: more of them go missing

Song of the Sky Llama: becomes even sadder

A Guildsman's strength: doubles beneath a Full Moon, quintuples beneath his Full Birth Moon, nonuples when his Full Birth Moon falls on his birth day

Luck: becomes more extreme

Jumping: happens more often

Animals: become more likely to embrace their artistic tendencies

When I pressed him to tell me more about Yewdu Wood and the Thundra, Yeti simply tried to distract me with a series of cartwheels. It worked. As always. I have not brought the subject up again.

Yeti is exceptionally impressed with my log book.

Not, alas, because of the insightful enscribblings already contained within its sea-battered pages. It is because he has never seen a book before! They do not have them on this island – at all.

Their stories are remembered and told by ancient chroniclers.

Their personal knowledge and experience is shared by word of mouth.

Their recipes are haphazard at best.

Their libraries are...well, they don't have libraries.

I think you get the point.

They do, however, have a form of enscribblment: highly ornate and as decorative as it is informative. Like painting, really. I have tried my hand at it and the results were uninspiring.

Luckily, Yeti has managed to dig out a quill (*a highly ornate feather unlike any I have seen before*) and supply of Octohead-ink, so I can scribble this log.

I shall learn more about this scribbling technique and report it later. For now, I am going to wash my beard in the sea.

The salt will help make it rugged. Possibly.

UPDATE

To be honest, the shock of finding myself on this island hasn't entirely worn off yet. It is especially intense being around Yeti all the time. He is a being of relentless energy – and it can be hard to keep pace with his enthusiasm for, well, everything.

I am not a shy person, but nor do I find it easy to relax in new social situations. This is one of the many reasons why I drink.

REASONS WHY I DRINK :

1. It makes me look better in boots.
2. It stops my punching hand from twitching nervously.
3. It makes me twice as funny and thrice as charming.
4. It helps me jump much higher. I think. → test this!
5. If I don't drink a thing, somebody less worthy might.
6. Over time, alcohol metabolises into ~~glory~~. → GLORY!

We have taken to dipping our glasses into the Sauce River at regular intervals throughout the day. This is normal for Yeti. He says sauce keeps him "perky." I cannot criticise. As we say in the Guild:

"Drink the spirits down: lift the spirits up."

Inevitably – probably because he was impressed by my ability to consume sauce, yet remain articulate, fleet of foot and capable of holding a tune – Yeti asked me what I drink back home. There was only one way to answer that question: I produced the Rumpass from somewhere within the folds of my robes.

In case you are unfamiliar with the Rumpass; it is a round fist-sized instrument with two spinning dials. One points towards mighty quests, rampaging beasts and feats of strength and daring. The other points towards the nearest rum.

It was created by combining two ancient tools: one that always pointed North and one that could detect water. Presumably the invention of the Rumpass made both these other devices obsolete: what would be their purpose these days?

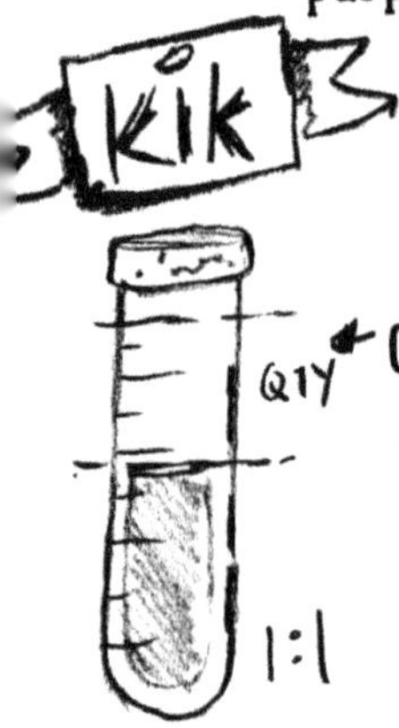

What most people don't realise is that the Rumpass also contains a small amount of Kik, the fabled and powerful rum of the Guild. Pouring Kik into the Rumpass is what activates its capacity for detecting more rum. It's like giving a hound the scent of its prey, or slapping a Guildsman around the face with a juicy steak.

I assume I can put anything into the Rumpass and it would have the same effect. I can't imagine why I'd bother, though: it already directs me towards quests and rum.

What else would I want to seek?

Maidens?

Perhaps. It sounds like an engineering nightmare.

THINGS I COULD PUT INTO THE RUMPASS

→ **CAKE:** the obvious second choice.

→ **KNOWLEDGE:** can one capture and contain and idea?

→ **STEAK:** a recipe for disappointment. Cows are not at all exciting. Unless they are marauding.

→ **MUSIC:** I once sang into a box. Then I sealed the box and delivered it to a fair maiden, as part of a juvenile courting ritual. She didn't offer me her hand in marriage. so I assumed it didn't work. Perhaps I just can't sing...

A cabbage merchant in Quaalpath once suggested we put some gold into the Rumpass and make our fortunes. I told her a Guildsman makes his own fortune. She said I had misunderstood, but by that point I was already neck-deep in a cabbage pie and couldn't hear a word she was saying. (*One eats cabbage pies upside-down. I have never asked why.*)

It has been years since that day, yet I still don't understand what she meant. Currently, the Rumpass takes me directly to rum. If it took me to gold, I'd have to mine the gold, smelt the gold, refine the gold, form the gold into some kind of...block, then spend it on buying somebody else's rum at inflated cost.

It would be a false economy.

Anyway, it was with great pride that I produced the Rumpass and let Yeti take a swig of Kik. He immediately leapt into the air and remained there, suspended, for a good few hours.

Everybody reacts differently when they first taste Kik. I am told I seized the Guildmaster, hefted him above my head and dropped into a deep squat. There I stayed, humming a perfect B-flat, for nine days and nights.

To his eternal credit, the Guildmaster refused to flinch for the entire time:

"Never interrupt a Rum Trance."

EVER

I had no idea how long Yeti's experience would last, so I made myself comfortable. When he eventually descended – in slow-motion, as it happened – I tried to demonstrate the navigational properties of the Rumpass.

Me

To my great dismay, I found the rum dial hanging limp! I feared the worst: it had suffered a break – or at least a sprain – during my marooning. I expressed my concerns to Yeti (*in the form of a long, mournful bellow*) and he put my mind at rest – in a sense – by informing me that he had never heard of rum before.

The Rumpass isn't broken; there is simply no rum around. I shall have to guard my supply carefully. A Guildsman without rum is like...well, anything without rum.

RUM

Much, much more tedious.

LOG ENTRY: FOUR

Viscous Waves

I was right about the sea. Yeti tells me it is well known for being bad tempered. I spent the latter half of today sitting on the beach, sketching the waves. They writhed unnaturally and smashed violently against the shore, as if it had challenged them to Punch Face. Gloves off, by the looks of things.

As the morning wore on, however, the tide seemed to calm. That was when Yeti pointed out the people in the sea, apparently riding the waves into submission – like mighty, frothing bulls.

"It's the Surferz Three, man! Gonzo, Bonzo and Alfonzo – they ride my enchanted boards. It calms the waves. Makes them all...flaccid."

I assumed he meant placid, but didn't investigate further...just in case. He was right, though. With a grace I wouldn't have believed possible, they balanced their boards upon the waves, gradually soothing them from furiously rolling breakers into harmless little whitecaps.

When I asked Yeti why they were wearing squid-shaped helmets, he almost wet himself laughing.

"*No no, man – they're Octoheadz!*" he told me, as if that explained anything.

(it didn't)

Before I could clarify, a wave managed to slip through th~~[illegible]~~z and **erupt** on the shoreline, hurling sand high into the air and sending Yeti scurrying for cover.

I let the sand rain down on me; it filled my adventuring boots to the brim and clogged up my sauce. I drank it anyway. It tasted awful. I don't know what I was expecting...

OTHER THINGS THAT TASTE AWFUL

- **WAKING UP AFTER "MESSA":** the Guild's feast to celebrate the rum harvest
- **LOSH'L:** the secretly-sourced 'dried meats' of Rononon
- **DEFEAT:** . . .
- **CAPEESH:** the bizarre Zoosgafistanian delicacy of rotting fish dipped in honey and fried in fermented cabbage oil
- **UNCOOKED WALRUS FACE.** Cooked walrus face is quite delicious. Like sugared plums.
- **CAT MILK:** milk for cats rather than the milk of cats, although I hear that isn't great either.

LOG ENTRY: FIVE The Sun

Yeti has promised to take me further into the island to meet a friend of his. He goes by the name Captain Awesome, so my expectations are fairly high. We leave tomorrow.

When I asked Yeti where the Captain lives, he gestured in a half a dozen vague directions. None were directly contradictory, but nor were they exactly complementary...

Apparently the islanders navigate by sheer luck and memory, as well as some badly constructed dirt tracks and a series of complicated routes that crisscross through the forests.

I tried to explain my technique of navigating by the sun and moon, but soon discovered that even they are different here. For one thing, they are the same thing!

I asked Yeti about the sun/moon.

"He's a strange guy, man." Yeti told me. *"Sometimes he's super happy and beaming, other times he's all depressed and stuff."*

He leaned close at that point, as if to whisper a secret.

"We think he's bi-solar."

I am starting to wonder whether I died in the shipwreck and have been reborn as a bearded baby on another world. At least I have my adventuring boots. With them, I can punt my way through anything.

I asked Yeti whether he could give me a map of the island. He answered with a solemn nod and a long, slow swing on his sauce. Then he sat in total silence. He is not very good at answering questions.

So be it. I shall draw up a map myself. It will be my parting gift to Yeti when I head back out to the open seas.

The search for the Great Extravaganza (*whatever that is*) can wait for a few days.

Can't it?

13-1

SMACK

YETI
STEEZ

LOG ENTRY: SIX
Post-Party Breakfeast

Yeti woke me late this morning to head out for the house of Captain Awesome.

To be honest, I don't think he slept. There was some kind of enormous beach party last night, complete with music, fire displays and competitions.

The last I saw of Yeti, he was flapping his flowery smock like wings and running into the sea yelling something about bears, hawks, hogs, skulls and victory. I like all those things, so I started to give chase.

Then I noticed he was heading towards what appeared to be a clash between two rival gangs, some riding boards and some riding complicated two-wheeled contraptions. I maintained my distance; *the introduction of a Guildsman into any brawl greatly alters the outcome, normally to everybody's detriment.*

QUOTH THE HANDBOOK

Instead, I went for a stroll through the party, drank some sauce and performed some feats of strength for the amusement of the islanders.

MY FEATS OF STRENGTH AT THE BEACH PARTY

Building and balancing a pyramid of Warebits (small, furry, toothy creatures) upon my head, then performing a perfect Guild Squat.

Leaping a pile of crates stacked as high as my own brow.

Out-arm-wrestling an Octohead: not easy because Octoheadz technically have 10 arms (two conventional arms, plus eight...head-tentacle...things).

Defeating an entire gang of Boneheadz at tug-o-war: easier than it sounds because Boneheadz, as their name implies, are not the smartest of people. (The Guild maintains that tug-of-war is really a battle of intellect.)

Quaffing a tankard of sauce whilst balancing upon my head.

Hurling a boot farther than anyone has ever hurled a boot: unverified (nobody could find the boot).

Eventually, I was awarded (or at least given) a very handsome hat. This is just as well, because my normal hat was lost in the shipwreck. Luckily, I managed to cling onto my Guild-issued secondary hat, which I normally wear upon my main hat to stop it from getting wet. It is called the 'meta-hat'.

The other inhabitants of the island are as bizarre as Yeti himself, if not more so. All of them wear gloves (*yet I haven't seen a single glove shop*). This seems odd, but I'm not having much luck getting sane answers out of Yeti. I shall wait and ask Captain Awesome.

Despite all his shenanigans last night, Yeti seemed quite chipper this morning when he roused me with a hunk of dried (and mysterious) meat and a tankard of sauce. After breakfeast, I performed my morning squats and had a hearty bellow. Some Guild customs must be maintained, even when washed up on a mysterious island.

We shall set off soon. Captain Awesome doesn't live far away, but Yeti wants to spend the afternoon handing out his newly carved boards to the Surferz on Vedwu Beach.

It will be a hard hike. I hope. I need a tough trudge to clear my head and stretch my lungs.

I already miss the sauce.

QUESTIONS FOR CAPTAIN AWESOME

WHAT IS WITH ALL THE STRANGE HELMETS?

WHAT WAS THAT GANG FIGHT ALL ABOUT?

WHAT IS ON THE OTHER SIDE OF THE MOUNTAINS?

WHY IS THE SEA SO ANGRY?

WHO OR WHAT IS YETI AND HOW DOES HE ENCHANT THINGS?

WHAT IS THE ~~SAFEST~~ WAY OFF THIS ISLAND? → MOST GLORIOUS

WHAT IS THE THUNDRA AND WHY IS YETI SO CONCERNED ABOUT CHOPPING MORE VEWDU WOOD FOR HIS BOARDS?

- × WHENCE COMETH THE SAUCE RIVER?
- × WILL THE SAUCE RIVER EVER STOP FLOWING?
- × IF SO, WHEN? IS THERE ANYTHING I CAN DO TO STOP THIS FROM HAPPENING?
- × IF NOT, IS THERE ANOTHER SAUCE RIVER ON THE ISLAND?
- × IF SO, WHERE?

→ IF NOT, CAN WE PLEASE GO BACK TO THE SAUCE RIVER?

HELP &
PROTECT!

LOG ENTRY: SEVEN

Meeting Captain Awesome

7

We have arrived at the house of Captain Awesome!

We got here around sunset and Yeti rapped on the door with gloved knuckles. It swung open almost immediately and there stood the Captain himself.

He is a large man, who filled the doorway despite being slightly stooped. He looked us up and down with piercing eyes, before finally nodding and retreating back into the house.

He tossed some chairs our way, filled some tankards with a foaming pitch black substance that looked and smelled like regret, then tossed those at us too. Then he folded himself onto a stool and stared at me across his ancient table.

It soon became clear that he was expecting some kind of explanation. I started by reciting my full list of deeds and titles, as befits a Guildsman.

Then I recounted my quest thus far, right from the moment when the Guildmaster sent me out in search of adventure and the Great Extravaganza (whatever that is).

As Yeti's request, I explained about the Nine Big Faces of the Guild: the paragons of Guildly virtue, by whose respective qualities every Guildsman aspires to live.

XXX

THE NINE BIG FACES

1. THE WRESTLER: a face much-punched, yet indomitable in combat. We invoke and wear this face whenever we find ourselves in need of courage or power. When performing a feat of strength, for example, or taking a bath. Hams Sally rarely takes this face off, not that he needs it.

2. THE OARSMAN: the grimace of sheer determination and iron will, invoked whenever we must endure great or extended adversity. I wore this face during my 95-day trek of the Pale Pass of Shadoom, for example. I also wore it whilst navigating my way to the puking trench, halfway through Quaffer Harris' birthday feast.

3. THE SMITH: the bearded visage of the patient, learned man of skill. We invoke this face whenever we must focus. We Guildsmen are not, after all, known for our ability to sit still and pay attention. Except during a rum tasting.

4. THE POET: the handsome and charming smile of the charismatic bard, invoked if we find ourselves in need of inspiration, creativity or a free drink. Or all three.

5. THE RANGER: the grizzled, wind-burned face of the explorer and hunter. This is the face we invoke when we embarking on a new quest, settling into a new environment or any time we must test our powers of self-reliance. I have been wearing this face since I washed up on this island. ever

6. THE REVELLER: the mischievous whisky grin that promises wicked tricks. This face ensures we remain in high spirits as often as possible and make the most of every situation. "The only difference between apart and being a party is 'Why?'" (Nobody truly understands that saying.)

7. THE STORM: the blurred face that represents the chaos we must embrace if we are to truly approach life in the most adventurous way possible. This is the face that glares at us any time our plans become too concrete, or we prepare too much for a feat. Once, I felt it snap at me for tying my boot laces too effectively.

8. THE FLAME: the flaming head of comradeship that guides us in all matters of hospitality and cordiality. You are always welcome at a Guildsman's fire. Unless you intend to put out the fire, in which case you will likely set aflame.

9. THE STRANGER: the shrouded face of mystery and the unknown, which comforts us in times of solitude, isolation and confusion. Like in a rum-out, for example.

Yeti interjected every minute or so to ask questions. He didn't understand the concept of "wearing a face", for example. I explained that it is a sort of meditation: the summoning and quelling of certain traits and mindsets, in order to constantly approach life in the most Guildly way.

“

For the most part, Captain Awesome listened quietly and slurped from his tankard. He shuffled with interest any time combat was mentioned and seemed particularly intrigued at Yeti's description of the Rumpass.

Leaping at my chance to impress this wizened veteran of the isle, I whipped out the Rumpass and poured Captain Awesome a generous serving of Kik.

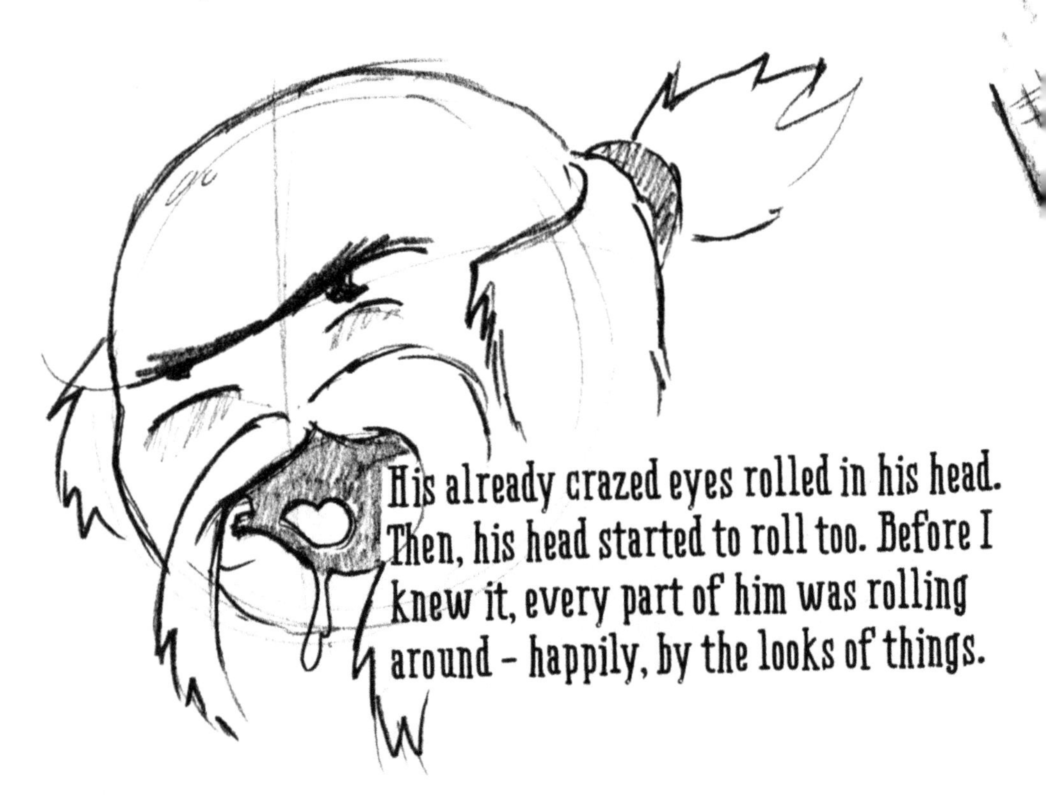

His already crazed eyes rolled in his head. Then, his head started to roll too. Before I knew it, every part of him was rolling around - happily, by the looks of things.

Eventually he stopped rolling and re...congealed. Then he leapt to his feet and declared, in a voice that sounded as though he was, at that exact moment, being punched in the liver:

"e must! To Ed!"

Then he passed out. And snored. Loudly enough that Yeti's tankard vibrated off the table and spilled its contents all over the floor. I couldn't help but notice the liquid bounce a few times, before it finally came to a rest in the rough shape of a puddle. This was concerning.

Whilst he was scraping up the mess (scraping is another word I have hitherto never associated with a drink), Yeti expanded upon Captain's Awesome's cryptic statement.

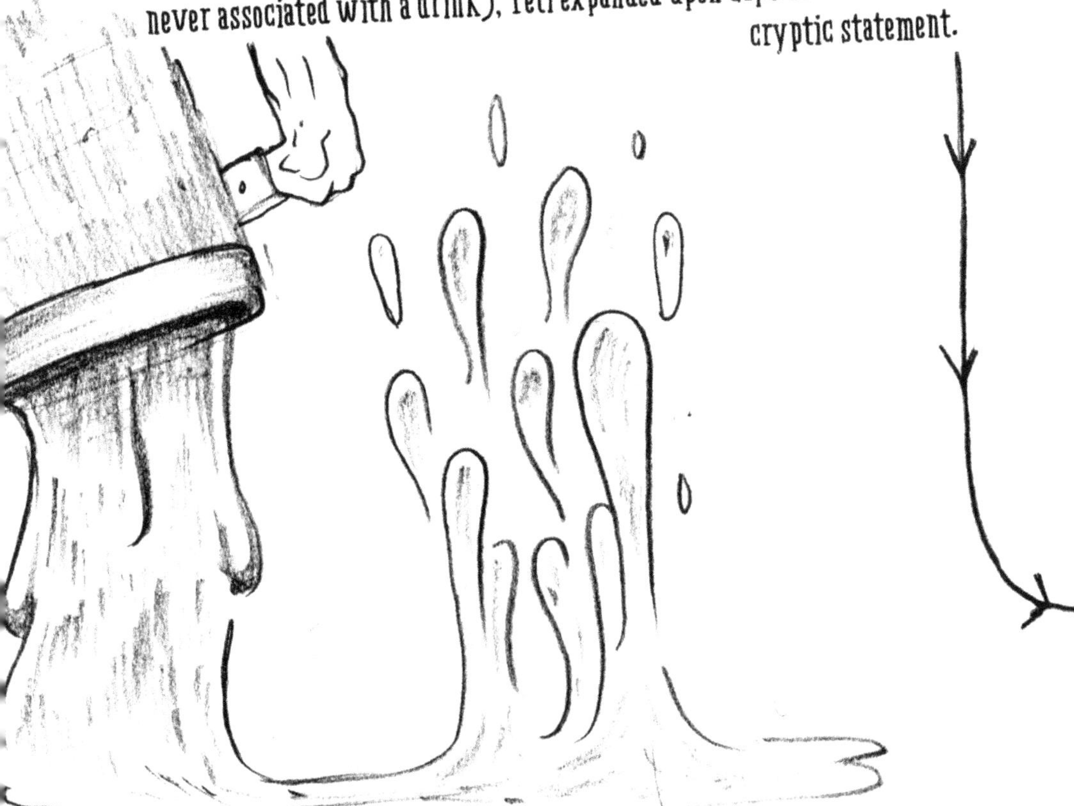

Ed was a reference to a chap called Metal Ed, who (*in Yeti's words*) "*loves, y'know... drinking and... adventure-y stuff*".

Captain Awesome is clearly of the opinion that Metal Ed would benefit from tasting Kik. This seems obvious: everybody benefits from trying Kik. Except for the unworthy, of course. They explode. Or worse: implode.

Yeti tells me that Ed, along with a number of other interesting characters, will be present at the forthcoming SkyFest – a musical gathering that takes places high in the mountains, "sometime next week".

Like their approach to navigation, the islanders are fairly unperturbed by timekeeping and calendar events in general. This suits me: a Guild plan rarely involves arriving anywhere – or anywhen – in particular. As we say:

> *"A Guildsman is never late, nor is he early. He decides when he means to arrive precisely when he arrives."*

Yeti and Captain Awesome are both going to SkyFest. They set out tomorrow morning and I have been invited to join them.

I am unsure. On the one hand, I enjoy music and mountains. On the other hand, I have been on this island longer than I expected, and the Great Extravaganza (whatever that is) won't find itself.

Or maybe it will. I genuinely have no idea.

What should a Guildsman do?

LOG ENTRY: EIGHT
Celebration Drinking

I have accepted the invitation to SkyFest. Captain Awesome has awoken (thank every one of the Nine Big Faces) and we have been drinking in celebration of our forthcoming journey into the mountains.

It wasn't an easy decision, but I'm sure the Great Extravaganza (*whatever that is*) isn't going anywhere for a few more days. Or maybe it is. Who knows?

For a while now, we have been swapping songs and telling tales. I attempted to get some more information about the Thundra, but both Captain Awesome and Yeti simply knocked their tankards loudly on the tabletop and changed the subject. ?

Luckily, I got a chance to finish my list of deeds and titles. It is important that I do this regularly, now that I have lost my Book of Deeds. I concluded the list with my role in the War Against Apathy.

At the mention of the word "war", Captain Awesome ~~had~~ looked up with a start. Then he slumped forwards and gripped the edge of the table, his eyes glazing over. For a moment, I feared he was suffering a rum-lapse! Then he spoke. At length. Here is an excerpt:

Finally, an

was nineteen, barely out of my baby clothes. Still, they took me anyway: gave me a
ece of rope and a tin of sardines, and there I was on the front line. 'Ten packs o' nine
hey paid in those days – and that was monthly! Of course, back then you could trade a
ickle for a ham and still have change enough for snak-snaks and sauce on the way
ome. Sauce was free, of course. But those were real snak-snaks back then: as thick
s your arm and heavy like wet clay – none of these trendy 'snakaroos' the kids are
nunching these days. It'll be the end of them, you mark my words. Although there are
ardly any words left any more, either – they used them all up in the Great
Discussion! Selfish, if you ask me. Is that still a word? Yes. Yes it must be. I just used
it. Didn't I? I don't suppose it matters. Still, if I was given half a chance – I wouldn't
need a whole chance, not that you can get them any more – I'd tell them EXACTLY
where they can put their debates! You know where that is? No? Well, let me tell you:
I was six years old – six or eleven – and I'd just finished my first solo night watch.
That was the custom, back then. None of this trendy childhood nonsense that all the
young 'uns are playing at..."

He has yet to stop this monologue. It feels like he has been speaking since the dawn of time, an event about which I fear he will provide a detailed account at any moment. I managed to feign interest for the first hour or so, but eventually decided that scribbling my log was a better use of my time.

Yeti is handling the situation far better than me, which hopefully means this is a normal occurrence and not another side effect of the Kik. He has just refilled our tankards of...drink, and is practising his yodelling. Captain Awesome doesn't seem to have noticed.

I shall go to bed soon, whether Captain Awesome has finished his story or not. Tomorrow, we take to the mountains.

ADVENTURE!

HOT!!
FLIP
KillER

LOG ENTRY: NINE

Breakfeasting

I awoke this morning to the smell of cooking meat. Captain Awesome was in his kitchen, frying up a storm.

This was music to my belly; much as I appreciated Yeti's beach-based diet, I hadn't had a decent breakfeast since the shipwreck. A Guildsman needs his breakfeast like a bear also needs its breakfeast.

→ NOTE TO SELF: *my similes suffer first thing in the morning.*

Rising quickly, I washed the sleep from my beard and joined Yeti at the table. There, the Captain dished up three kinds of unidentifiable (*yet delicious*) meat, eggs aplenty (*I didn't ask from which creatures they came*) and a variety of flora of differing densities.

All this and more he piled high upon our plates, until I could feel my stomach straining against my ribs – intent on bursting free and devouring the entire world!

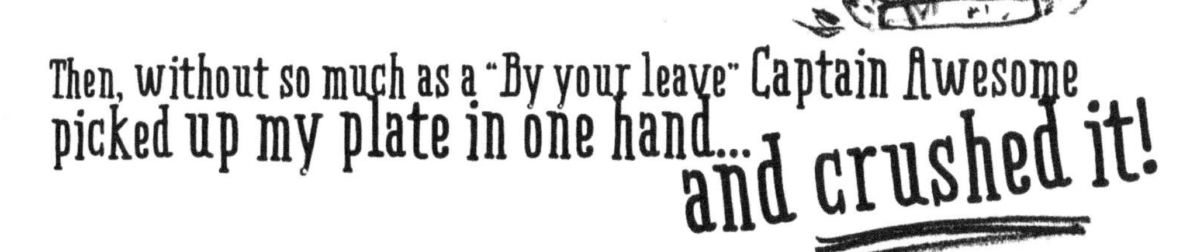

Then, without so much as a "By your leave" Captain Awesome picked up my plate in one hand... **and crushed it!**

My horror was absolute.

Yeti tells me I leapt – from sitting – into the air without my feet touching the ground, screaming all the while. No such fate should befall a breakfeast! I don't remember if I openly wept, but when my vision finally cleared I noticed that both other breakfeasts had disappeared as well. Never had I known such rampant inhumanity.

With a heavy heart, I accepted a new and awful realisation: **I was going to have to murder Captain Awesome. With my napkin.** This is the only reasonable way to respond when you have just witnessed the crime of feast breaking.

Luckily, Yeti sensed the danger and placed a hand on my shoulder. Then he picked up a squishy ball the size of my head, and took an enormous bite. All suddenly became clear.

In my morning grogginess, I hadn't noticed that our plates were made out of some kind of dough. With a twist and a yank, the Captain had turned my disorganised pile of food into a self-contained unit of breakfeast.

It was the closest thing to genius I have witnessed since the Guildmaster opened a bottle of rum by bellowing at it.

AMAZING FEATS I HAVE WITNESSED:

→ Hams Sally breaking the record for the heaviest squat, by squatting the existing record-holder whilst he was in the process of breaking his own record.

→ The Master of Ceremonies out-fighting half a dozen picked men back to back, whilst suffering from a terrible case of Bjorliga: the condition of being incapable of standing from drinking too much beer.

→ The Guildmaster beating himself in a tug of war.

→ O' Kluz visibly growing his beard through willpower alone. When his nose started to bleed, not one person in the room believed he would continue, let alone succeed.

→ Sneaky Feet Pete sitting perfectly still for an entire month to disprove allegations that he was stealing sheep to make himself a fine hat. No sheep were stolen during that time. He was sentenced to Trial by Cake and lost.

(This log is starting to make the Guild sound like simpletons).

ACTS OF TERRORISM I HAVE WITNESSED

× The Hammer pouring away the dregs of a barrel of Kik, "for the sake of us all".

× Hams Sally singing anything!

× Red Red Steve tying Elbows Shelly's boot laces together, so she failed to leap over the proving log and had to re-sit her entire jumping qualification.

× Jane o' Blades hiding a family of badgers in The Master of Ceremonies bellowing girdle, on the first morning of Sprung – when we all ~~take~~ sing the Sprung Song.

I apologised to my companions for my emotional reaction and blamed it on sauce withdrawal. Then I tucked into my breakfeast...thingy. It was delicious: like honey and rainbows covered in joy, except with meat instead of honey, meat instead of rainbows and meat sauce instead of joy.

For the record, I don't fully understand the difference between meat sauce and joy.

Is one the end and the other the...means?

If so, does one justify the other?

And **which one is which?**

SO MANY QUESTIONS!

To accompany our breakfeast wraps, there were two types of toasted bread: crusty wholemeal for the men and sweet white for the ladies. Being as there were no ladies present, we ate both.

We washed everything down steaming mugs of an invigorating concoction called smokin' bean brew. It was equal parts sweet and salty, and made me want to jump, fight and weep all at once.

We are just waiting for Captain Awesome to finish the washing up. Then we shall heft our packs and set out for the Twisted Peaks.

ADVENTURE awaits!

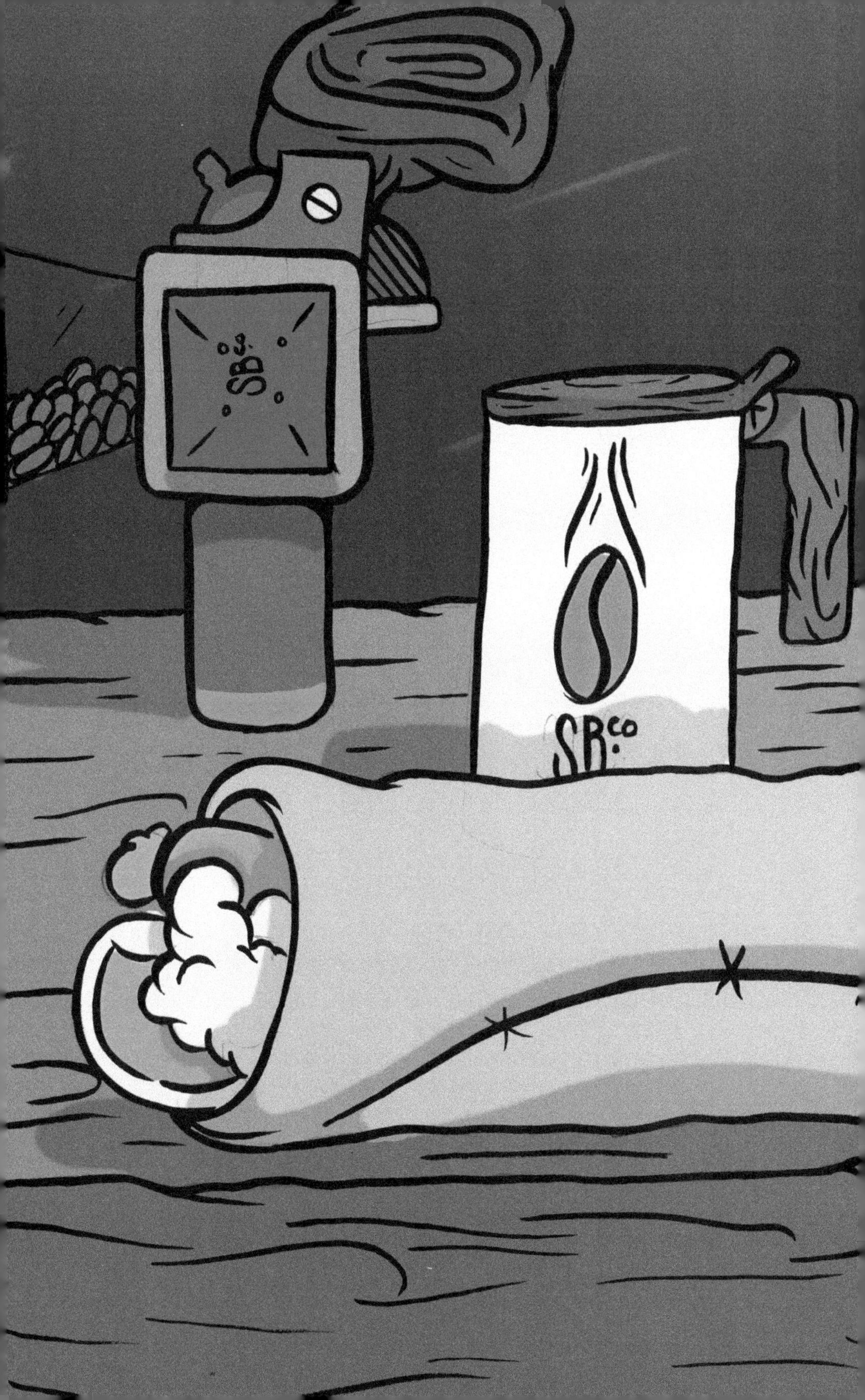
SB
SB co

LOG ENTRY: TEN
Re-Outfitting

We have stopped by the town on our way to the mountains. The Captain informs me it is called the Happy Ghetto, which is a curious name if I have ever heard one – and I have heard one. In fact, I have heard many:

CURIOUS NAMES I HAVE HEARD:

TOOTHY BAN-AHN: richest (and ugliest) spice merchant in Eastern Quaalpath

TELE-MUTTONFACE: owner of Trumpets Mega-Warehouse. Not to be trusted.

BRAVERY JONES: infamous Goddess of Plenty, to whom I lost my fourth and final virginity

SIX O'CLOCK AND THE PONTOON BAND: chieftain of the Buk side of the Triangular Plains of Tal-Buk-Tol

S'OPA-INFACTR: the skittish, one-eyed elephant I rode during the land-based stage of the Great Ham Race

VISROPEN WISE-WISEST: shaman of the Uncomfortable Twins (two small rocks behind my local cabbage distillery)

FLK QTTLRRRK: boat taxi driver on the Helta Delta who only accepts payment in the form of dance. Does not give change.

LOOFUS P. PLOOPUS: cyclist, barber, legend. Travels fastest when hopping.

That reminds me. The name of the island is

The Isle of the Vewdududez.

If anything, that's even stranger than the Happy Ghetto.

But who am I to judge these things? I, Codename.

According to Captain Awesome, it used to have another name.
Whenever he tries to remember it, however, he lapses into tales of yore.
It is never worth the risk.

Having lost almost everything I own in the shipwreck, I have been thoroughly re-outfitted by Yeti. It turns out he owns a shop called the Vewdu Store, where he sells just about everything an adventurer like myself could need.

When we arrived, Yeti gestured at my sea-ravaged robes:

"You can't go into the mountains in a dress. You'll freeze! Or be mocked to death."

I tried to explain that a Guildsman fears neither cold nor fashion, but it was too late. In a whirlwind of hair and cross-stitching, Yeti's helper, Geoff (or Ge-Off, as Yeti insists on calling him) had assembled - and somehow dressed me - in brand new adventuring attire!

He even managed to find gear in the Guild colours of red (*the colour of fire, rage and the blood of our foes*) and black (*the colour of rum and the night, which we typically fill with rum*).

Ve
VEWDU
SHOPE

SCOPE

Most amazingly of all, it fits! Like most Guildsmen, I struggle to find clothing that fits my brutally practical physique. We are not exactly cut out to strut in the High Fashion Houses of Quaalpath. Or even to strut the Low Fashion Houses.

We are not really cut out to strut.

Yeti and Captain Awesome may be large fellows, but the average islander – whilst being roughly my height – is not of a similar shape to your humble, yet undeniably rectangular narrator.

They typically lack the dense, knotted musculature of a Guildsman. In fact, in the case of the Boneheadz, they lack any musculature at all!

VEWDU ADVENTURING GEAR

SMOCK: warm and hooded, as every good smock should be. It is not as waterproof as my Guild robes (it lacks years of careful oiling), but I can wear it beneath them for extra warmth and comfort – and padding, in case I should receive an unexpected gut-punch.

TROOS: thick and tough, yet loose around the knees and balls – where a Guildsman moves most. A plethora of pockets means I can also effectively lose a variety of equipment upon my person, for untimely rediscovery at a later date.

I SURF!

HELMET: however brawny his arms, the most valuable part of any Guildsman is his head. How else can he deliver a killing blow without spilling his rum? Yeti's helmets come complete with storage straps for keeping essentials as close to your face as possible. Yeti keeps a paintbrush, Captain Awesome keeps his pipe. I shall keep my log book and perhaps a stylish feather. I shall need to find a stylish bird. (Now I think about it, my quill will do the job nicely.)

CASUAL ATTIRE: a selection of comfortable tunics, doublets and pantaloons for the times when I am not roaming the wilds. Each piece is emblazoned with some of Yeti's own unique artwork. I am not yet certain how he will feel when I chop the arms off these tops, but Guild traditions must be maintained.

LEATHER ARMOUR: simple lightweight armour for the mobile adventurer. It is unlikely to stop a well-placed shank and would be utterly hopeless in an axe battle, but it will prove excellent for bear-hugging lively Java Foxes and the other minor skirmishes one encounters in the wild.

CLAMBERING TWINE: finally, something I recognise! Long pieces of study rope, primarily used for climbing up rock faces, but also useful for settling disputes in the age-old Guild fashion: the tug of war known as GRIP. The presence of these ropes and buckles in my kit sack is both exciting and slightly arousing.

AXES: Yeti has honoured me with the gift of one of his enchanted Yewdu Axes. I don't quite know how to repay the favour, but I must remember that I already gave him some Kik – so perhaps we are now equal. He also gave me a couple of smaller axes. They designed for hacking my way up mountains, but I fairly sure I can dual-wield them in Berserker Style if we suddenly find ourselves at war in the coming days. As the Guildmaster says:

"Never leave home unarmed; you cannot feel a battle in your bones. Not until afterwards, anyway."

FOOT CLAWS: any Guildsman worth his Swashbuckles can kick his way up an icy mountain. Descending it with grace, however, often takes the clever use of boot-spikes like these. They also serve a self-defensive purpose: nothing ends a scuffle quicker than a spike-clad boot to the gonads. That is why I always wear a protective codpiece. (That and the fact that it is the height of fashion. I assume.)

BOARD: a piece of Vewdu wood with wheels poking out of the top. The learned Smith himself can only guess what this contraption is for, but Yeti is clearly very proud of it. It would not be polite to turn down such a gift.

I insisted upon keeping my own boots. Like the men who wear them, Guild boots only get tougher and more leathery over time. Rumour has it that after a decade of solid wear, they even sprout beards! I don't believe this.

NOTE TO SELF: attempt to covertly investigate the boots of the older members of the Guild for the existence of beards. Perhaps pose as a boot-shining service.

At the moment, Yeti and Captain Awesome are arguing over which combination of smoking herbs they will take for the journey.

I am drinking more smokin' bean brew and breaking-in my new adventuring pantaloons. I don't want to chafe in the coming hours.

NOTE TO SELF: scrap boot-shining idea. "A Guildsman's boots should never be cleaner than his face".

LOG ENTRY: ELEVEN
The Golden Horn

Due to having replaced my breakfeast rum with half a gallon of bean brew, I have just nipped for my fifth pre-adventure urination. During the process, I noticed something glittering in the undergrowth.

I stopped urinating temporarily to scoop it up (such is the enviable bladder control of a Guildsman) and it appeared to be a horn of some kind: golden, curled and – surprisingly – hollow. It looked quite valuable but, before I could give it much more consideration, The Captain was roaring that it was time to set off.

I have shoved the horn into my new adventuring pack. With the tug of adventure now firmly about my loins, I shall don the Face of the Ranger and set off at a Guildsman's pace!

Twice the pace of a normal man.

With thrice the bellowing!

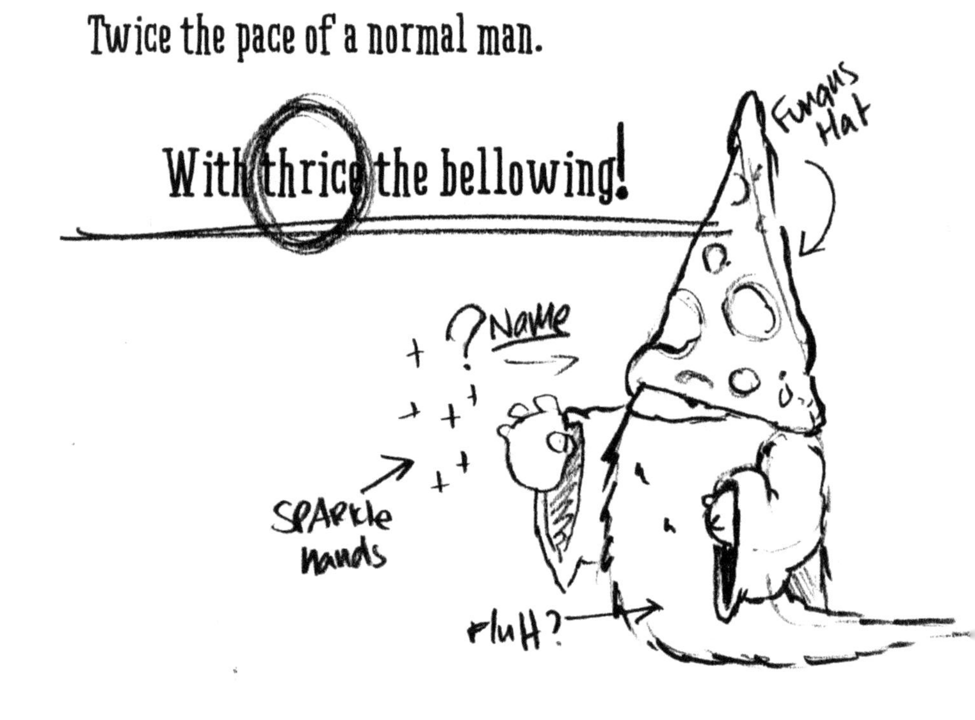

SHHH!

LOG ENTRY: TWELVE
Slow Progress

I am becoming concerned that it will take us all week to reach the mountains, let alone climb up to SkyFest.

The fact that I can enscribble this whilst walking is a fairly good indication of the pace that Captain Awesome has set.

I would call it "leisurely at best."

I knew the islanders were relaxed in their approach to time keeping and navigation, but this is ridiculous. If the Guildmaster was here, he would be furious:

"YOU'D GET THERE FASTER WALKING BACKWARDS!"

He would bellow, much to everybody's confusion.

THINGS THAT WOULD MOVE FASTER THAN US

A three-legged dog carrying a bigger dog

A wheelbarrow being pushed by a distracted penguin

A beginner ice skater, who is also a cat

A fox, trotting

A flamingo, foxtrotting

A fox, doing the flamenco

Any two animals engaged in a dance-off

A man with arms for legs (not, however, a man with legs for arms – like the Guildmaster)

An inflated balloon fired from a crossbow

I have given up trying to maintain the face of the intrepid Ranger. Instead, I am concentrating on the face of the Reveller: the man who can endure anything with a smile.

It is nice to be out and about, walking through the woods.

Nevertheless, I am starting to think the tug of adventure I felt in my loins was actually just the need to urinate, yet again.

Curse that bean brew.

I am getting rather frustrated with carrying around this leather armour, helmet and confounded wheelie-board!

It is a cumbersome burden - **and for what?**

The others simply do not seem to understand the question: when I ask, they simply puff on their pipes, mutter about routes and gesture into the distance.

They have been discussing which island beast is the most ferocious and powerful. Yeti claims the Bearkhawk is the most terrible beast on the island: **half bear, half hawk - all terror!**

Captain Awesome maintains that the Bearhawk is a myth and that the Great Grey Mape (apparently the largest of the Mapes) is the most powerful beast in the land.

Apparently when the Great Grey Mape sings, clouds gather - and rain eventually falls.

Yeti scoffed at this claim and stated that, if the Bearhawk doesn't exist, then the Big Fuzz is the largest and, therefore, most powerful beast.

This conversation is very interesting, but it isn't hastening our journey.

I may try lunging instead of walking. It would be worthwhile exercise if nothing else.

LOG ENTRY: THIRTEEN Roots?!

Captain Awesome is power-monologuing again, so I am taking the opportunity to update my logbook in case I die in the coming minutes. Allow me to explain.

Our morning stroll came to a halt at some kind of canal. At first glance, it looked like a riverbed. Upon closer inspection, I realised it was actually made of the subterranean boughs of the surrounding trees, all knotted and interwoven.

It makes me think of a giant beard, tangled and matted from lack of grooming. And made of wood. The name Jumble Woodbeard springs to mind...

which I believe might be a cousin of mine. Or perhaps my second wife.

I forget

so much these days.

Somehow, presumably thorough an extended period of growing, hewing and polishing, this twisted mess has been carved into a vast system of smooth interlocking channels, which link the different parts of the island together.

These are the pathways by which the islanders travel. The organic alleyways.

The roots.

I get it now.

This one has a name: Root Sixty Sticks.

Of course.

The roots themselves are not what concerns me, however. It is the method by which one travels them.

Yeti was first into the root. Without even a backward glance, he hefted his wheelie board, tossed it into the chasm, and – with a series of highly coordinated manoeuvres that I honestly hadn't expected a Sasquatch to be capable of performing – he leapt onto the moving board.

Bellowing something that reminded me very much of battle cry of the Lam-Phon-Lanian Scarf Warriors, he careered down the side of the root, up the other side and away into the distance!

I wasn't convinced. I must admit I tried to talk my way out of it, by explaining at length to Captain Awesome that a Guildsman needs only his legs and a supply of rum to travel any distance. Rumming, we call it. At Guild pace I'd be there in a few days.

"You have to trust the board, son. It will keep you safe."

Such were his words. I told him a Guildsman keeps himself safe – mainly by not leaping into obviously fatal situations. He chided me:

"Nonsense. The Vewdu boards know the way Folk have been using them to navigate the roots for as long as anybody can remember. Why, my old milk man used to deliver the milk by root every morning and never spill a drop! Of course, that was before the war..."

Before I could intercede, he was off:

"Every morning he came. Henry was his name. We used to leave a tip for him under a sack of yams. Of course, yams were worth more than money back then, so we used to hide the sack of yams beneath a bigger sack of yams, but replace the yams with lumps of coal! Now I think about it, coal was much more expensive than yams in those days... But nobody knew that the sack was full of coal, you see, because it looked like it was full of yams! Oh yes, we knew how to make a plan in those days – imm ediate action! None of this 'thinking' nonsense that all the kids think is so fashionable..."

He hasn't stopped yet. I am starting to think he never will.

Escape is becoming an increasingly tempting option...Is it truly bravery to perform a courageous deed, simply to escape something even more terrifying?

Is now the time to don the Face of the Wrestler, for courage?

Or am I committing myself to the cause of chaos – should I don the Face of the Storm?

Can I don half of each face?

As we say back home:

"Let's not over-think this":

FOR THE GUILD!

BASE CAMP

LOG ENTRY: FOURTEEN
Root Sixty Sticks

I am alive. I am not sure how. As that awful old saying goes:

"The Stranger works in stranger ways". 

My chances of staying on that tiny board with all my gear as it rocketed down the side of the root were as good as non-existent. Yet, like The Captain had promised before getting lost in the archives of his memory, the board seemed to read my mind and kept me perfectly balanced the whole time.

I may have looked like a giraffe under heavy artillery fire, but I felt safe... Ish... Safeish.

That's about as good as it gets, being a Guildsman.

Even so, riding the board will still come fairly high on my list of tricky skills I have learned:

Other Tricky Skills :

- Leap-frogging the giant leaping frogs of Bur-Bad-a-Dad
- Posing as a lily patch to escape the Horse Lords of Trembloy
- Milking the udders of the Great Sky Cow
- Out-running the nine-legged horse known as Terrible Shu
- Shaving the face of Taramandu without waking any of his sixteen children
- Striking the one weak point in a Guildsman's mass of abs
- Singing the Song that Ends All Things
- Helping to maintain the health of the Guildmaster, by convincing him that fruits are the eggs of very exotic animals

Sure enough, the board also knew the way. Every time it connected with a new root, it would swing me onto what I could only assume was the correct path. Occasionally, I could have sworn I was actually travelling uphill!

Eventually, I came across Yeti picnicking on the side of a root and, through a combination of clenching and gurning that I intuitively and immediately dubbed 'clurnching', I managed to bring my board to a stop.

Captain Awesome has yet to appear, so I am taking the opportunity to introduce Yeti to the concept of a Rum Lunch. It's like lunch, but with more rum.
It's almost exclusively rum, in fact. No wait, it IS exclusively rum.

But at lunch time.

For lunch.

A rum lunch.

I believe it is working.

LOG ENTRY: ~~FIFTEEN~~ Rum Lunch!!!

Captain Awesome is here now too. He is a nice man. He rides his board with grace. Also, he can blow smoke from his nose – HIS NOSE, can you believe it? I can't believe it. Well, I can – but I can't believe I can believe it.

Does that make sense? Yes Yes I think it does

This rum lunch is a good 'un. My brain has become very foggy indeed. I am trying to tell Captain Awesome about the time I milked the Sky Cow, but he thinks it is a rude story and has closed his ears.

Yeti finds the story funny. He asks why he cannot see the udders of the Sky Cow, if they are so large. I don't know... Perhaps they are invisible udders. We should ask her – the Sky Cow I mean.

"Sky Cow...are you

That's what we'll say. Of course, we'll have to find her first.

FIVE THINGS I AM BETTER AT AFTER RUM LIST

1. Scribbling bleak poetry about Days of Yore.

3. Baking snakes. I mean cakes – or snacks. Or do I? Can you bake a snake? I expect so. because it is very fun to say.

5. Singing of MY DEEDS! Like when I milked the invisible Sky Cow.

5. The fandango.

5. Hopskitching

9. Seasoning to taste

2. Times tables. e.g. 4 x 6, 9 x 6, and 317 x 6 (Answers are 24. 54 and approx. 1900)

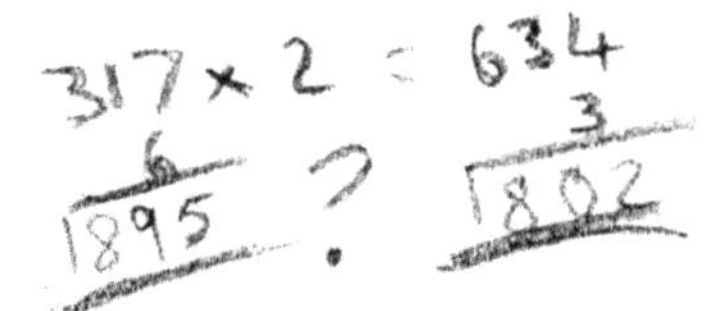

scribbling myself down a
song. A song about a hero!
Called. Hero Steve.

HERO STEVE,
HERO STEVE,
HE WAS A HERO!
HE WAS A STEVE!
HERE HE COMES,

HERO STEVE,

HERE HE COMES,

visible?"
HERE AND HE

LEAVES!

Goodness. I cannot scribble songs after a rum lunch. Who knew?
Most of the time, I am better at things after rum:

Whoops, we are leaving!

Once more onto the board: it's still scary even after rum!

FOR THE RUM!

I mean the Guild.

FOR THE GUILD.

LOG ENTRY: SIXTEEN
Cake-Cake

Let us never speak of Rum Lunch again. It should be between friends.

And never documented.

The sun has dipped below the mountains, so we have made camp for the night. Yeti has made a dinner of Cake-Cake.

"*It's like a cake made of cakes...*" he explained.

It tastes a lot like cake. Luckily, I like cake.
I'll **PUNCH** any man who says otherwise.

Tomorrow, we will reach the Twisted Peaks.

The fresh mountain air may help clear my head.

LOG ENTRY: SEVENTEEN Crumch

Morning has broken. To repair it, we've turned to a combination of cake-cake and Rum Lunch. The result is somewhere between a cake lunch and a rum cake. It's nothing like a rum-rum, however.

It shall call it Crumch. POWERFUL and TERRIFYING, like a...

...whale.

Before us, the Twisted Peaks rise. Soon we shall ditch our boards and continue on foot.

Judging by my Rum Lunch Ramblings of yesterday, I do not trust myself to enscribble anything for a while.

Not after Crumch.

LOG ENTRY: EIGHTEEN
Base Camp and the Portawheel

I am in a place called Base Camp. It is a village of canvas erected high up in the Twisted Peaks. From my tent I can see a mighty stage – the setting for tomorrow's musical performance.

I have taken a break from the festivities to scribble in my log. You can probably tell. TI has been some time since I last scribbled, so there is much to tell. I should at least document some of my journey here before the constant revelry inevitably obliterates my memory.

Once out of the Ghetto Pines, we trudged our way to an enormous contraption called a Portawheel. Now, as a Guildsman, I use the word 'enormous' with startling regularity. When talking about breakfeast, for example. I also use it to describe my beard, quadriceps and ceremonial codpiece.

When I say this Portawheel was enormous, however, I mean it was

ENORMOUS.

Imagine the height of a man.

Now imagine the height of ten men, standing on each other's burly shoulders. You're nowhere near.

Imagine one hundred men, somehow standing upon each other's heads. With their boots on. That is roughly the height – or diameter – of the Portawheel, give or take a few of those men falling during the process of building such a human tower.

The whole thing is fixed to the side of the mountain by a giant pole. Now, as a Guildsman, I use the word 'giant' with startling regularity...

There is no tree – real or imaginary – giant enough to create that fixing pole. Not even the combined girth of ten trees, plus both Hams Sally's legs, would even come close to matching the size of it. The Smith himself could only forge such a thing, I'd wager.

Half the Portawheel sits beneath a rampaging waterfall that plummets down the side of the mountain. As the stream strikes the slats of the wheel, it spins. On the other half the wheel, where the slats are rising, bold adventurers such as ourselves can leap aboard the wheel and be transported upwards.

At the top, one simply springs clear and finds oneself high up in the mountains with the minimum of effort. Simple. In fact, there are only two down-sides to the Portawheel. One of which is...well, the down side. If you miss the exit point because, for example, you are mid-feast, or asleep, or simply a fool, you quickly find yourself being tipped upside-down to meet what I assume is a grisly and undignified demise.

The other downside is that few things are harder than coordinating a fully-laden leap onto a moving contraption made of slippery wood. Especially after a hearty Crumch.

Luckily, I survived the leap.

You may have noticed.

Once safely off the Portawheel, we began what I expected would be a good old fashioned hike-up-the-mountain-trail. Excitedly, I hefted my pack and braced my calves for a-shredding, but Captain Awesome flagged me down before I work up a good pace.

"Don't be foolish, lad. Let the board do the hard work!"

With that, he dumped his pack and gear onto his wheelie board and strolled off up the mountain trail without it. Assuming he was having a senior moment, I jogged over to scoop up his equipment for him. After all, a pair of Guildsman's legs can bear twice the burden of the average pair. Remember that, next time you're out leg-shopping.

Before I could touch the pack, however, the board jolted as if I had kicked it in the back of the knees. Not that it has any knees. Then, apparently of its own accord, it started following Captain Awesome along the path!

I have come to accept the oddities of this land, but watching a wheeled board carrying a pile of adventuring gear up the side of a mountain was verging on the insane. To start with, I assumed it was simply a side-effect of the Rum Lunch. Or a dream. To double check, I punched myself in the face.

It was no dream. Or, if it was, it was vivid enough that I should treat it with the same respect as reality - if not more.

So it was that I loaded up my board and followed the others up the path. Sure enough, the boards followed us the whole way! For a while, Yeti even perched on the top of his gear, smoking his pipe and singing to himself as his board effortlessly transported him into the mountains.

I did not try such tricks. A magic board it may be, but the only thing that carries a Guildsman up a mountain is his own two legs.

Or a Phoenix.

10 Things I Would Let Carry Me Up a Mountain

1. A flaming lion
2. Two smouldering lions
3. The wings of love
4. An eagle wearing a hawk as a helmet
5. A noble stag
6. The jackal
7. Twin panthers
8. A mastodon
9. An albino version of any of the above
10. Another Guildsman, in an emergency

We arrived at Base Camp that evening and my memory of the next couple of days is even more of a blur than usual. This place reminds me of the Great Party of Quaalpath, but colder and with fewer teeth.

I shall endeavour to keep up my log.

large ears
* Bright red
Soft Fur & Markings
Small Nose
Small Mouth

LOG ENTRY: NINETEEN
Billy Psycho

From what I have just learned over breakfeast, however, it is much more than a music performance: it is something of a ceremonial ritual. According to Yeti, each of the Twisted Peaks is actually an active volcano!

If they aren't appeased, they:

"Erupt and explode and all kinds of crazy stuff, man! It gets real messy. Real messy. Like...whoa!" ǂ

For years, the inhabitants of the island tried just about everything to keep the volcanoes under control: regular sacrifices, poetry-reading, home-baking... Yet it turned out the only thing that can soothe them was music. Loud, aggressive music – as it happens.

That's where a man named Billy Psycho comes into things. Or so Captain Awesome told me as he performed his morning squats. *(I have been teaching Captain Awesome some Guild customs. He is taking to them with vigour!)*

"By regularly performing in the peaks, Billy keeps the volcanoes soothed and entertained, so they don't feel the need to cook us all their their amusement."

Yeti chimed in at that point.

"He's like the Surfers Three, dude! Keeping the waves all flaccid for us."

I'm thinking back to my first day on the beach and trying to imagine what it would have been like if, instead of waves crashing violently on the shore and showering me in sand, it had been lava cascading down these mountains and covering me in...well, lava.

It is disturbingly easy.

I have yet to meet Billy Psycho, but I'm already grateful for his existence. Goodness only knows what things were like before he turned up.

A lot hotter, I expect.

ǂ At this point in his explanation, Yeti waved his hands around mysteriously and his pipe traced a smoky pattern in the morning air.

LOG ENTRY: TWENTY
Meeting Metal Ed

Captain Awesome joined me for lunch in the feasting tent this afternoon. He was in particularly high spirits, which he attributes to the 'mountain air'.

"It reminds me of the days when I used to take the guys out running the trails!"

He told me, thumping the table so hard that our tankards leapt into the air.

"Of course, back then there weren't any paths or steps: we just ran straight across the rocks, leaping like gazelles! Manly gazelles, of course. I'd take a long-spear and we'd hunt for boar during the afternoons. Nothing like flame-roasted boar to put the strength back in a man's legs. Such legs we used to have in those days..."

Suddenly, something burst into the room. On its knees.
It was...power-sliding?

Before it had even slowed to a halt, it leapt to its feet
in a typhoon of hair and fists and bellowed:

"SAUCE!"

I don't know why, it may have been my inherent lust for danger or perhaps the need to excuse myself from Captain's Awesome's reminiscing, but for some reason I handed the figure my tankard.

It snatched it from my grasp and, in one swift motion, swallowed the lot!
I haven't seen liquid disappear as quickly since last time I went fishing with Quaffer Harris!

BREW
DEATH
BY
HEROISM
XXX

"SWEET DELIGHT! I AM SAVED!"

the figure boomed and, falling to one knee at my feet, it raised the empty tankard above its shaggy head: "Fair maiden, I am forever indebted to you for this kindness."

I opened my beard to explain that I was no maiden, but a grizzled veteran of the Guild of Adventurers. Snapping out of his reminiscing, The Captain cut me off:

"Use your eyes, man! The two you have left, anyway... This is no maiden! This is a grizzled..."

"If it is no maiden..." the figure interrupted, poking a meaty finger at my Guild-issued breakfeasting robes, *"Why is it wearing a dress?"*

That was a step too far. Power-slide into my feasting tent, quaff my drink and confuse me for a maiden – fine, if you must. Insult my Guild robes, however, and you have a duel on your hands! Or your fists, to be specific.

My first punch landed squarely on his chin. The second hammered into his temple and my third was a cheeky shot to the gut – a classic Guild combination. For a moment, nothing happened. Then a split appeared in the front of his head, parting his beard like a hairy earthquake...with teeth. He was smiling.

"Alexander McCuba", Captain Awesome addressed me, *"Meet Metal Ed."*

In one swift motion, Ed pulled me into a vice-like bearhug and shook me until my spine made a sound like two trees vigorously mating.
(I have heard this sound only twice, and I hope to never hear it again. The trees, I mean. Not the cracking spine: I have heard that sound innumerable times and, actually, it brings me great pleasure.)

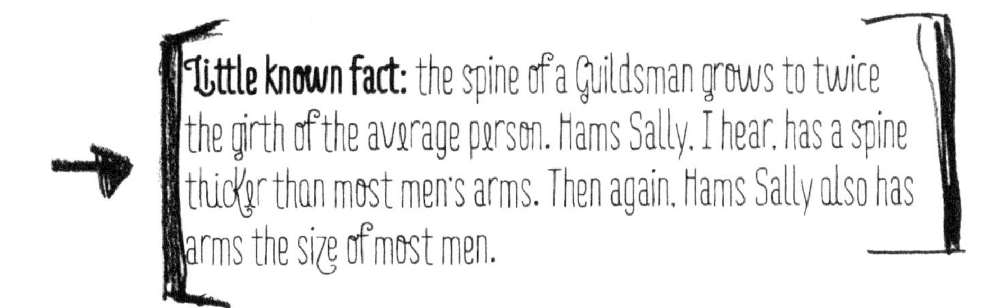

Eventually, Metal Ed let me go and pumped his fists in the air in celebration – apparently pleased to have started his day with some kind of violence. That was when I noticed his right hand; there was a significant chunk taken out of it where his smallest knuckle should have been.

He must have noticed my gaze, because he looked me dead in the eye, razed his fist aloft and roared: *"Punched the lightning, didn't I? Punched it right out of the sky!"*

He leapt onto the table, scattering foodstuffs with his booted feet. Snatching up another tankard, he upended it over his head and blew a great cloud of droplets into the air.

"IT WAS A DARK AND STORMY NIGHT..."
he bellowed, somehow managing to fix everyone in the room in his gaze at once.

This man, I realised, was a Guildsman. Whether he knew it or not.
He probably did not.

What followed was a highly detailed – perhaps suspiciously highly detailed – account of the time when Ed fought a storm in the mountains. According to the man himself (and nobody was disagreeing), the storm had mocked Ed's moustache.

"Of course, I challenged it to single combat – of course, of course! Yet though I faced IT, it did not face ME...for the storm has NO FACE!"

He leapt into the air and came crashing back down on the feasting table, creating a mushroom cloud of actual mushrooms.

"No face I tell you! How can a man fight something that has no face?"

He looked me dead in the eye:

"HOW CAN A MAN PUNCH THAT WHICH DOES NOT EXIST?"

He had a point.

At the end of his tale, Ed ripped his shirt, tore at his hair and wept – before slumping into silence. I started to applaud, but realised everybody else had already continued with their lunch. Apparently this display was nothing out of the ordinary. By the time I had gathered my wits, Ed was already fist-deep in a chicken.

Thus was lunch on the sixth day. We have now commenced the pre-festival drinking, so I must leave this log for the time-being. I shall take it with me to the gig, however, and document every passing moment in case all goes awry and the mountains wake up and burn us all to a cinder.

If this happens, I shall wrap this log book in a soggy shirt and hide it beneath a rock.

That should do the trick.

LOG ENTRY: TWENTY-ONE
Arriving at SkyFest

The time has finally come!!

We have left the comfort of the breakfeasting / feasting / drinking hall, crossed the entire length of Base Camp and gathered around the stage for the SkyFest musical performance.

There is no set-up of any kind. No instruments that I can see. No sign that anything is about to happen at all. If it wasn't for the gathering around the stage babbling excitedly, I would wager we have come on the wrong day!

I feel a bit light-headed. It might be the mountain air.
It might be the ale.
It might be the excitement.

It might be all three!

Or two of three.

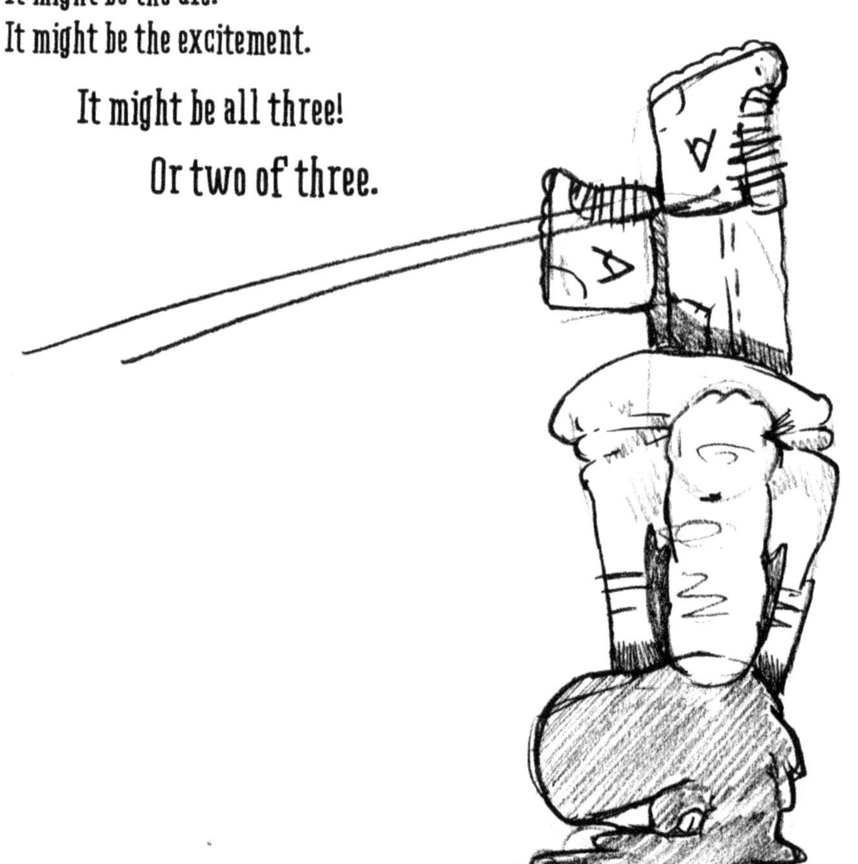

OTHER THINGS THAT MAKE ME LIGHT HEADED

- A good ol' fashioned uppercut.
- A fifth o' scrum: the rum / scrumpy combination that famously blinded One-Eyed Jack.
- Complex Guildgebra: the abstract calculations used to determine glory, honour and the feat/deed distinction, amongst other things.
- An extended beardstand.
- Jogging
- Peace

The stage itself is a mighty wooden structure, nestled so snugly in its rocky crook that it appears to be part of the mountain itself.

In fact, parts of the mountain actually intrude onto the stage like props: either the stage has been built around the mountain or the mountain itself had grown over the stage. I have a fairly good idea which is the case, but I have learned not to assume anything here.

The general set-up and ambiance remind me very much of Deed Peak, where Guildsmen have gathered to take their vows of adventure beneath the full moon since time immemorial.

Billy Phycho

Irritatingly, this festival situation is giving rise to what I believe are my first twangs of homesickness...

It is a strange feeling, much like weakness – or how I remember weakness felt, back when I suffered with such things.

It is similar to the feeling of longing for rum after a hard day at the forge, or the total opposite of landing a solid hook punch.

I find myself in conflict – and not the good, bloody kind either. This strange land is fascinating and baffling, and I am yet to even scratch the surface of what it has to offer. Adventure abounds and I, as a representative of the Guild, am duty-bound to delve deeper!

Yet this search for the Great Extravaganza (*whatever that is*) has already taken me far and wide. It has been many a moon since I last feasted with my brothers and sisters, or supped from the Horn of Adventure and Rebirth.

I do not know if it is Guildly to feel homesick, so I have consulted my Guild Handbook for guidance:

↓ ↓ ↓

> *"Like the Ranger himself, a Guildsman is at home in any environment. He is never more at home, however, than when he is – actually – at home."*

As mystifying as it is enlightening. Thus, the Guild.

Still, at least I have Yeti and Captain Awesome for company. Metal Ed, on the other hand, has disappeared. He better show up soon, or he'll miss the Show!

LOG ENTRY: TWENTY-TWO Happy Memories

Metal Ed has appeared. On the stage!

He is standing square in the middle of it, behind one of the shorter lumps of mountain, legs spread wide apart. He is slowly raising his hands to the sky and clenching them into fists.

"Power stance, dude!" Yeti has just whispered excitedly in my ear.

Dark clouds are gathering overhead. I do believe that, before my very eyes, Ed's fists are actually starting to grow! He is still drawing breath – perhaps a speech is forthcoming...

Or a rousing chorus of Drinking With Steve! I haven't sung that song since the last Feast of the Cold Moon, when the Master of Ceremonies sang a verse which went on so long that The Hammer was forced to tackle him from the bellowing plinth.

Of course, Grip ensued. (*The one-handed tug of war that settles all Guild disputes.*) The Master of Ceremonies was furious. If I remember correctly, he punched The Hammer so hard he went blind! Temporarily, of course.

It was a brutal match, that one. By the end, most of us put The Hammer's grip down to rigor mortis. Imagine our surprise when he leaped from the ground to execute a one-legged spinning hip toss, which gave him the split-second opening he needed to tear the Grip Rope from the hands of the Master of Ceremonies. He later named the move La Flamenco.

It took days before somebody plucked up the courage to tell The Hammer that he had confused ornithology and dance. Of course, Grip ensued...

Ah, I could reminisce on the Guild all evening if there wasn't a performance to be witnessed. I should wrap things up:

OTHER FOND MEMORIES OF THE GUILD :

→ When the Master of Ceremonies pulverised a cantaloupe, skin and all! Or was in an antelope? I forget now, it was so long ago.

→ The Duke of Prateesh punching Quaffer Harris so hard that he blinded himself.

→ Danny Two-Brains and Jane O' Blades boating the wrong way around the Proving Lake and having to start all over again.

→ Rumpunsel letting down her golden beard

→ When the Guildmaster first experienced doubt, and challenged himself to Grip.

→ Watching The Hammer slow dancing after the Rum Harvest.

→ When Hams Sally nearly maimed everybody at once by tossing us a basket of month-old quick breads, thus inspiring the creation of the deadly doubled-sided Throwing Biscuit.

Good times.

My homesickness has re-redoubled.

INHALE

LOG ENTRY: TWENTY-THREE

METAL ED SINGS?

Metal Ed is still drawing breath. It has been some minutes...

I am becoming concerned that he may be about to sing the Song to End All Things!

It could still be Drinking With Steve, however. Some people take longer than others to come up with a verse. Why, sometimes even Estoniatus takes his time ascending the plinth and some say his lyrics come from the quill of the Poet himself.

[That has jogged my memory: I have played Drinking With Steve since the Feast of the Cold Moon; I played it aboard the Great Ship Ass. By myself. It wasn't the same.

The group chorus was especially pointless.]

Still Metal Ed draws breath.
Do the others know about the Song to End All Things?

I may have to storm the stage and save the world.

Again.

LOG ENTRY: TWENTY-FOUR
Storm

Huge relief: Metal Ed is not singing the Song to End All Things. He is...yodelling?

Mournful and haunting, the sound is bouncing off the surrounding mountains and being magnified a hundred times over. The entire area is reverberating!

It is like receiving a Quaffer Harris full body massage, except marginally less terrifying.

(This particular memory has helped alleviate the homesickness somewhat.)

Lightning has started to flash across the sky. From somewhere very close by, thunder is swelling and roaring as if the storm itself is trying to sing along with Ed.

The homesickness is back again and worse than ever. Music in a storm? Estoniatus would kick himself if he knew he was missing this - and probably cripple himself in the process. His are the quadriceps that broke the Mega-Metre, after all.

I must stop reminiscing now; it is not doing me any good.

Yeti and Captain Awesome are warming up. I should join them. I shall scribble more when the performance has reached whatever kind of conclusion follows a storm-based introduction.

LOG ENTRY: TWENTY-FIVE
After the Skyfest

I hurt. Everywhere: from my fingers to my soul. The performance this evening was like nothing I have ever witnessed. Now I am safely back in the Feasting Hall, I shall do my best to give an account:

As soon as the thunder and lightning started, Captain Awesome gave a start. Glancing up at the skies, he clapped his hands excitedly, rolled up his breeches and started to perform some deep squats, his knees cracking ominously. Following suit, Yeti commenced bouncing up and down, shaking out his long hairy limbs and rotating his head.

Never one to ignore the importance of a warm-up, I gyrated slowly to loosen my hips and performed a few quick beard-stretches. Nothing interrupts a performance like a moustache strain.

Before I could check that my adventuring boots were appropriately lashed to my feet, Metal Ed brought his magically-enhanced hands crashing down on the rock in front of him with a booming crunch. Beneath his massive fists, the ground shook as he started to pound out a beat to accompany his yodelling. The crowd erupted into life. (Not literally, thank goodness. I was still very nervous about the volcanic situation at this point).

"*Here we go!*" Yeti yelped excitedly and bent down to help Captain Awesome up from his final squat. He had gone too deep.

DUKE

At that moment, a sudden streak of lightning shot over our heads and struck the top of the stage in an explosion of wood-chips. A cloud of smoke quickly engulfed the entire stage and, from somewhere inside that cloud, a slender man strode out. I remember thinking to myself: did he just...ride the lightening?

This, without any doubt, was Billy Psycho. In one hand, he held what appeared to be a kind of lute. In the other hand, he brandished a long cable. With great ceremony, he held one end of the cable aloft and, mouthing what were no doubt some very sacred words, plugged the cable into his instrument.

A great cheer rose up from the crowd and, without knowing why, I joined in. It seemed churlish to remain silent when everybody else was convinced something important had just happened.

Then, with an even greater degree of aplomb, Billy strode to another part of the mountain that was jutting onto the stage and, somehow, attached the other end of his cable to the rock. Finally, he held his instrument up above his head.

For a moment, nothing happened. Then, in an eruption of blue lightning that seemed to originate from Ed's fist, Billy's guitar started to writhe and flash. Immediately, Billy leaped into the air, powerslid (powerslided?) across the stage and struck his instrument. The sound hit me like Hams Sally when I poke fun at his mono-brow.

Somehow, Billy Psycho was using the mountain itself to amplify the sound of his instrument. From somewhere, Metal Ed had snatched up a curious type of horn and was using it to amplify his yodelling to a now deafening volume.

And just like that, the crowd came to life. Together, the usually laid-back people of the island surged forwards and, somehow, upwards! I tried to stand my ground, but it was futile. Even the sturdiest of Guildsmen would have been swept away in the tide.

DUKE

Seeing my comrades rapidly disappearing into the crowd, my only choice was to submit to the movement of the mass. Automatically, my hands grasped for oars, a rudder – anything to control myself in this sea of bodies. Alas, all I succeeding in grabbing was a facial tentacle of a nearby Octohead, who was not impressed at all.

Clenching my hands into fists by my side, I drew a deep breath and donned the Face of the Wrestler. I sought courage and strength. Something to help me survive the crush... For a few moments, all I felt was an elbow in my ribs. Then, slowly, peace returned to me...and I relaxed.

From then on, it was beautiful. When we jumped, we jumped as one. When we landed, the ground below us shook. This, I realised, must be how it feels to be a sausage amidst a hearty breakfeast: a tiny part of something much bigger and more important than myself.

Overall, I did The Reveller proud. I may also have shortened my lifespan by a decade or so. Luckily, I know a trader in Quaalpath who does great discount rates on livers. I'll have to send him a message when I find a way off this island.

I must leave this entry for now; Metal Ed has just exploded into the room with an enormous wooden barrel over his shoulders.

I believe the party is about to begin!

Reveller see me through.

LOG ENTRY: TWENTY-SIX
The After Party

By the Guildmaster's balls, I am in such pain.

Bizarrely, my memory of last night is crystal clear – up to a certain point. After that, I remember absolutely nothing at all. It is as if somebody reached into my head and removed my brain for 12 hours or so.

I remember cheering as Metal Ed dumped his barrel on the ground. I also remember joining the jostling queue of people eager to fill their tankards. Most clearly of all, I remember the awkward look on Ed's face when I reached the front of the line. I heard Captain Awesome's voice in my ear:

"My fine adventurer. I'm afraid I cannot let you drink from this barrel. This Voo Brew is dangerous stuff, truly. In the wrong belly, it can turn to fire and ice – searing the viscera and melting the guts into a sort of...stew."

He scrunched his eyes shut and shook his face violently. It made a sound like a sneezing bloodhound. Then he wiped the spittle from his mouth and gestured to the assembled company.

"Everybody here is an anointed member of the WVWF: the World Vewdu Wrestling Federation. Each of us has been tried and tested in the heat of battle and finally deemed worthy of drinking a concoction such as this. If would be neither safe nor wise to let you imbibe."

I understood: certain customs must be upheld. This was common practise amongst the Guild as well; only the most stalwart and decorated of Guildsmen were invited to test their bowels when the first experimental batch of Kik was unleashed. Many still died that day.

I remember telling them honestly: *"It is no matter. I was just looking for an excuse to try out my new drinking horn"* and tugging forth the golden horn I had found in the bushes back in VewduDudez Ville.

Immediately, the atmosphere changed: there was a bustle of activity and, suddenly, the air was glittering around me. Every member of the WVWF was waving aloft his own golden drink horn! They were of greatly varying size and shape, but all equally resplendent.

"We have misjudged you, McCuba" Metal Ed intoned, severely; "If you can rip a golden horn from the head of a Rammen, you are more than worthy to drink of the Voo Brew!"

Then everybody was cheering and, before I knew it, I was hoisted into the air and ceremonially carried over to the barrel so I could fill my horn. The fact that I was already standing next to the barrel and therefore only moved a matter of inches didn't matter: it was the thought that counted.

I am not proud of what I am about to scribble down next, but a Guildsman always tells the truth. Or rather, a Guildsman normally tells the truth...except when the truth is particularly inconvenient and will get in the way of a party of some kind. Party first, truth later.

In short, I did not tell the WVWF how I actually came across the horn. I would have spoiled their fun if I mentioned that I'd picked it up off the ground whilst urinating.

I should have probably given it a wash... Oh well, too late now.

Instead, I raised the horn above my head, plunged it deep into the barrel of Voo Brew, drew it out and – summoning my best Guild bellow – quaffed the lot!

The rest of the night is a mystery.

I can scribble no more down for now. My head feels like a thumping sack (the large bags full of rocks, against which we Guildsmen practise our face-punching).

I can barely hold my quill, and the words are starting to swim before my eyes.

If this is just a hangover, it is unlike any I have ever known.

It feels more like dëath.

I would know.

LOG ENTRY: TWENTY-SEVEN
Voo Brew: An Investigation

As a Guildsman, I am proud of my capacity to drink – or indeed to consume just about anything and turn the accumulated energy into mighty deeds.

Whatever the WVWF was drinking the other night, however,

may have killed me.

All Guildsmen are familiar with death. I am more accustomed to it than most, of course, having died a few times in the course of my duty.

Other than death itself, however, this is the closest thing I have experienced to being deceased since I was forced to journey to the underworld itself to claim back some tax.

The Guild owes no tax for we rely on very little that is external to our order. In fact, we have recently starting imposing our own Deed Tax: 40% of the gross estimated pre-deed loss (after deduction of a good will allowance) plus expenses. The proceeds (be it gold, glory or distressed maidens) normally go directly towards funding our rumery.

I spent most of yesterday abed, arduously enscribbling my last log entry. I had to stop every few moments to dry wretch or, even worse, wet wretch. When I could scribble no more, I fell into a strange fever dream that seemed to last a lifetime. I cannot remember what it was about now, only that something or someone has stolen one of my legs.

A seal, perhaps. With wings?

I awoke in a cold sweat to find bread and water by my bedside. I wolfed both down and immediately felt awful. Eventually, however, I summoned the testicular fortitude to haul myself from my squalid canvas prison and crawl around Base Camp, trying to find out what the Voo Brew is made of:

What follows are my findings, collected from various interviews:

METAL ED:

"IT'S THE TEARS OF THE GODS! THEY WEPT WHEN THEY REALISED OUR MIGHT!"

What followed was a song, which I simply couldn't jot down quickly enough. It was greatly entertaining, but almost certainly not true. For one thing, it contained the rousing chorus line:

WE PUNCH THE GODS! WE PUNCH THE GODS!
TOGETHER NOW, WE PUNCH THE GODS!

...which, frankly, I disbelieve on multiple different levels. I also took the chance to ask Metal Ed about the Thundra. He replied by clapping me on the back, laughing shortly and wandering off, humming "*We punch the Gods*".

BILLY PSYCHO:

"It comes from the other side of the island, man – the Thundra. Over there, everything works backwards and all the waterfalls fall upwards from the ground! When the fruits fall from the trees, they all shoot off in random directions like POW POW POW POW POW POW..."

At this point, Billy got over-excited and started shredding on his very expensive air-lute, so I left him to it.

CAPTAIN AWESOME:

"It was the Year of the Buffalo. Back then eggs were real eggs and bigger than your head. The chickens were bigger too, now I think about it. I suppose they had to be. Anyway, it was an unusually long spring that year, which meant summer had to get a bit of a move on. I don't recall if there was time for July, but August certainly came around much sooner than any of us expected. We weren't ready, you know. Not at all. I told them: "Dereks" I said – we were all called Derek back then – "Dereks, we're not prepared!" Of course, they didn't listen. They had to have the last laugh. Oh, how we laughed back then. The jokes were bigger, you see. Longer, too. Some of them took weeks to tell! How did that one go? You know the one – about the whale. Oh yes: what's a whale's favourite dance? Eh? Oh I can't remember. Can you? Some kind of waltz, probably."

This interview continued for some time after I stopped making notes. It may have lasted long after I left, too.

YETI:

"It's magical mead, man! Nobody knowns whence it came... or whence it goeth...to..."

At this point, Yeti started waving his hands around to convey mystery and the unknown. He refused to talk any more.

This is getting me nowhere.

BEARHAWK.
SBC

LOG ENTRY: TWENTY-EIGHT
A Sacrifice

My investigation into the contents of the Voo Brew has stalled. Much like their attitude towards the other side of the island (the Thundra), everybody's feelings towards the Brew seems to be that ignorance is bliss.

That simply isn't good enough. The only thing that is bliss to a Guildsman is a well-placed punch to the throat or the relief that follows the fleeting nausea of putting your foot down onto a stair which doesn't exist.

I have therefore resolved to conduct my own investigation into this substance using whatever suitable apparatus is available to me. I shall check my gear.

There is no suitable apparatus available to me. Nothing but my own, long-suffering liver.

So be it. Reveller protect me; I shall drink once more of the Voo Brew and attempt to document the experience in this log book.

If I don't make it out the other side, remember me as a scientist and man of exceptional mental girth.

I have managed to lever the lid from the barrel using one of my ice axes, but the Brew levels have dropped too low for me to reach down and fill my horn. There is only one thing for it.

I'm going in. **FOR THE GUILD!**

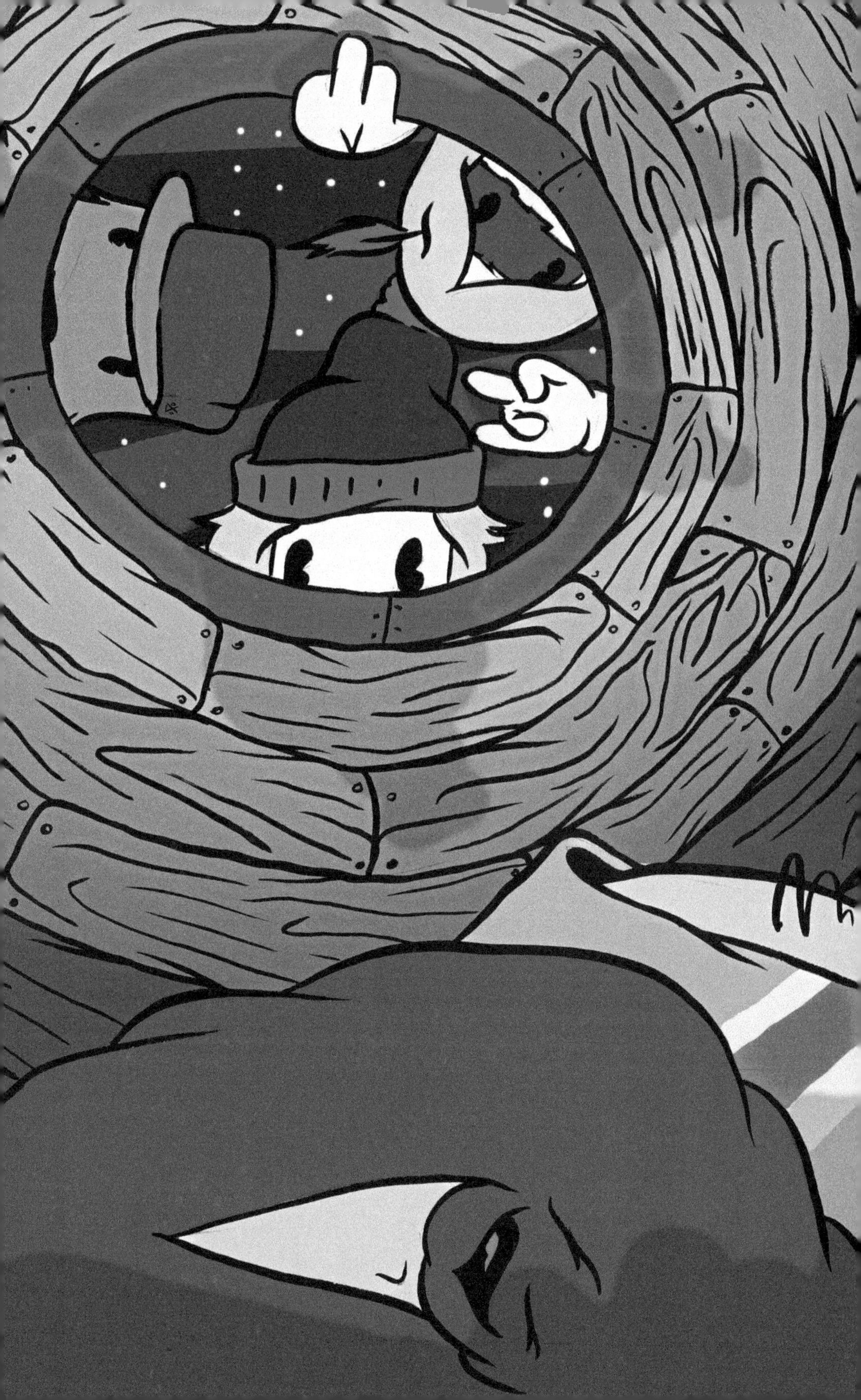

LOG ENTRY: TWENTY-NINE
Voo Brew: Tasting Notes

What follows are a collection of tasting notes I apparently scratched into the side of a tree last night.

Using my teeth.

APPEARANCE:

Lots. Everywhere! Treacly ocean that ONLY I CAN CROSS! Has a current – forms habits. Shifty: nervous or deliberately misleading – always plotting. What are your plans, sweet liquid pain? Looks like thunder.

TASTE:

TREES AND MADNESS! Sweetened lava melting into Earthy terror: planet itself reaching upwards to CHOKE ME OUT! Screams cut short by sudden, unstoppable inward collapse: reveals caramel if caramel is a variety of PUNCH TO THE MOLARS! Too-slowly morphs into stinging wood-smoke, reminiscent of a village burning.

Fresh explosions. Twang of omnipresence. Terrifying mix of hysteria and trepidation: promise of glory without happy ending. A challenge – A CHALLENGE MET! Faintest hint of Dragon Tears...or mustard. A deep sniff makes eyes water like an uppercut.

MOUTHFEEL:

Initial stabbing through epiglottis quickly contorts into merciless bludgeoning of entire body. Inverts tongue: leaves certain twinge of regret somewhere around base of spine. Hides teeth from the back, no remorse. (The rest of this entry is illegible).

FINISH:

Long. Very long. Too long. WILL IT EVER END?! Everything and nothing: lingering sense of loss hanging over a battlefield, centuries after fighting has ceased. Ebbing return like the tide. Hint of peach. BY THE GODS. MAKE IT STOP!!!!

I have no recollection of scribbling them and they have taken a number of hours to decipher.

I have a faint recollection of crawling into my tent, unzipping my skin and burying my head. There, I clenched my buttocks and braced for the hangover.

I woke up in a tree.

I am still in that tree.

LOG ENTRY: THIRTY
An Awful Morning

This morning has been awful. It started when Metal Ed "helped" me out of the tree by punching it down. Until I witnessed it first-hand (*or first-fist*), I didn't believe such a thing was possible.

Shortly afterwards, Captain Awesome shoved one of his breakfeast wraps into my mouth and Yeti declared we were going for a walk through the mountains. Normally, this would be my ideal hangover cure, but I was struggling with the worst case of Bjorliga have ever experienced.

For a short period, I tried walking on my hands. It didn't work out well; the rush of blood to my beard was almost overwhelming.

I should point out that I was upside down at the time, not just walking with my hands beneath my boots. I have tried that before and it is both painful and strenuous on the lower back. It is, however, an excellent way to develop good knuckle-calluses for punching things and...well, punching other things.

Eventually, Metal Ed suggested I lie on my Vewdu Board and let it transport me. That was the final embarrassment: "the chalk that snapped the lifting bar", as some say in the Guild. I tossed my Log Book in his general direction and referred him to my *List of Things I Would Let Carry Me Up A Mountain.*

(ENTRY 18)

Then I hauled myself to my feet (*by clinging onto what turned out to be parts of Yeti*) and, placing one adventuring boot in front of the other, I slowly collapsed.

Ten minutes later, however, I was back on my feet and ready for action.

That is more than can be said for the rest of the group, who are still milling around gathering up their possessions.

Apparently they are taking me SURFING: the art of wave-riding, as I witnessed on the beach. Of all the things to do with a hangover, I can think of few less enjoyable.

Luckily, there is no sea to be seen so, unless they are expecting me to ride my waves of nausea, I think they might be joking.

To make the journey slightly more bearable, I have armed myself with a stout walking staff and an even stouter stout.

As we say in the Guild:

(I cannot remember what we say in the Guild.)

Such is the hangover.

LOG ENTRY: THIRTY-ONE
Arriving at Lake Mayhem

We have arrived at a place called Lake Mayhem, high in the mountains. It is, as you can probably guess, a lake. Yet what its name belies is its exceptional beauty. It is enormous, blue-green and surrounded by snowy peaks. Bizarrely, for a place named Mayhem, it is totally placid.

Perhaps I am missing something, but this doesn't seem like the ideal spot for surfing. I may have misunderstood the central concept, but my understanding of the art of wave-riding requires...well, waves. ??

My memory of the walk here is nothing but a blur: the shuffle of feet, the perpetual need to vomit, and the occasional song to raise our spirits – in the form of Billy Psycho's twanging lute or Metal Ed's bellowing.

I fear I may have poisoned myself.

Yeti has a small wooden hut here, which he calls the Board Shack. It is overflowing with boards, gear and wetsuits of all shapes and sizes. It is a lovely day today, but I can imagine is gets pretty cold in these mountain lakes in the winter. If there is a winter here...

We aren't the only ones at the lake, either. There are a handful of Octoheadz at the shack, who seem to spend most their time drinking, waxing boards and sun-bathing. Despite their company, Yeti has sworn me to secrecy:

> *"You must never – ever – tell anybody else about Lake Mayhem, man. I'm serious: this is our little secret. Just us guys, you and the dudes in the Board Shack over there. Oh and the Surfers Three, naturally."*

He nodded towards Gonzo, Bonzo and Alfonzo, who bowed. I wasn't sure how to react, so I bowed back. They seemed pleased.

We are to sleep in a bunk house. It isn't the comfiest place in the world, but it has a bar. On the downside, it only serves drinks that Octoheadz enjoy. On the plus side, it turns out Octoheadz have pretty good taste in drink!

You just have to gargle it a bit first. And not breathe through your nose for a few seconds after you swallow. And not let yourself anywhere near a naked flame for at least an hour.

I know what you're thinking. And yes, I wasn't intending on drinking. I have realised, however, that I am sharing a bunkhouse with Captain Awesome...or Captain Snoresome, as he should be called.

That's actually pretty funny: I'll tell him tomorrow.

I firmly believe that drinking myself to sleep is the only way to sleep through his noise.

THINGS I HAVE SLEPT THROUGH :

- The Great Cheese Quake
- Stamp Eid: the Feast to celebrate the end of the postage strike
- A large portion of the Great Ham Wars
- My own birth
- The fifteenth verse of Estoniatus' epic during "Drinking with Steve"

SNORE!!!

LOG ENTRY: THIRTY-TWO
Anything Pizza

I feel much better today! I believe it was thanks to my breakfeast.

Captain Awesome (his new nickname didn't catch on) assembled everybody around a very curious-looking contraption this morning. It looked how I imagine a kiln would look if it decided to retrain as a hair dresser.

> "There is only one breakfeast suitable for a hard day on the waves..." he announced whilst limbering up with a borderline explicit series of bends and lunges.

It is called Anything Pizza. As the name suggests, it is a pizza topped with absolutely anything – hence the need for the incredi-kiln that works as a pizza oven. Captain Awesome, for example, likes to smother his with a sense of pride, add thick-cut slices of war story and roll the whole thing up into some kind of narrative roulade. He assures me it is delicious.

Yeti tries something different every time. Today he asked for unicorn steak and high expectations, with a lock-picking sauce and spicy chiliagons. I assume this is what he received, but none of us had the faintest idea what any of that should taste like, so I suppose we'll never know for sure.

Billy Psycho enjoys a melodic sauce with a scattering of riffs and a crust stuffed with harmonies. Today he requested an extra serving of solo over the top. Shredded, of course.

Metal Ed places an Anything Pizza upside-down on top of another to create an Anything Pizza sandwich. The actual filling is a mystery, but rumour has it that if you leave the Anything Pizza Sandwich alone with other pizzas, it will eventually absorb and annihilate them.

When it came to my turn, I ordered an Anything Pizza topped with another Anything Pizza, which was also topped with another Anything Pizza – and so on to create an infinite-regress of pizza, each separated by a thin layer of dipping-hubris.

What I received was a friendly warning-punch to the kidneys.

I changed my order to a classic Guild Barbecue: a burly base of black rye, covered with a rich ale sauce and topped with beef steak for strength, lamb shank for endurance and (*some say ironically*) chicken hearts for courage. Crack a dozen eggs over the top, douse in rum, set aflame and leave to smoulder at the top of a mountain. Some recipes should never be tampered with.

This evening, I think I'll try a base of bravery tinged with recklessness, topped with a tangy glory sauce and decorated with my many deeds. I may garnish with some freshly-grated feats of daring.

IN↓
INCREDSKILN
50
100
0
XXX

LOG ENTRY: THIRTY-THREE
A Summoning

I arrived by the side of the lake this morning just in time to see the Octoheadz producing and hefting their enchanted Vewdu axes.

Yeti winked at me and clapped his huge hands together with soft thumps, as the Octoheadz gathered in a circle by the lake. There, they extended their arms out in front of them, palms up with their axes lying gently in their grasp.

Facial tentacles wriggling solemnly, they raised their heads to the sky and started to croon. Nothing happened for a minute or two then, ever so subtlety, I noticed their axes had started to...sparkle, for lack of a better word.

Just as I was wondering whether I was still hallucinating from the Voo Brew, the axes slowly began to rise up into the air and convulse! I glanced at Metal Ed, just to be sure I wasn't seeing things. He grinned at me. That didn't really clarify the situation. Before I could ask a question, however, the lake started to grumble and churn.

I was already en garde, but when the lake erupted in a tower of turquoise water I still jumped about a foot into the air. For a split second, I saw something: most of it looked like a shark, but it was the size of a whale!

Immediately, I felt the blood rush to my fists:

I MUST SLAY THIS BEAST!

Luckily, Metal Ed held me back by the base of my beard because, moments later, the monster surfaced again to reveal that, along with gargantuan proportions, it had another abnormality:

the head of a squid?!

Yeti leapt for joy..???!

"They've done it, dude! They've summoned the Sharktopus! Time to hit the lake!"

The Sharktopus. A giant, lake-dwelling, mountain Sharktopus. I cannot possibly see how this has helped our situation.

If anything, now we can't even go paddling in this lake!

These people are insane.

I need to get off this island as soon as possible and resume my quest for adventure!

LOG ENTRY: THIRTY-FOUR Sharktopus Surfing

After the summoning of the Sharktopus, I spent the remainder of the morning kicking back in a hammock. It hangs between two Arockakaikai, otherwise known as the 'Moshing Palm Trees'.

For the most part, their rhythmic movement is relaxing and soothing to my hangover. Occasionally they get a bit carried away, presumably in the climax of whichever un-hearable song they are moshing along to. At these moments, I tend to vacate the hammock, fetch myself a cool drink from the Board Shack and watch the action on the lake.

It's quite clever, actually. The Octoheadz seem to have some kind of kinship or friendship with the Sharktopus and, after a bit of chin-wagging (or whatever they have instead of chins) and a bit of waving around their enchanted axes, they have persuaded it to help them out.

Essentially, by using its vast bulk to agitate the waters, the Sharktopus creates a variety of water-based obstacles. Sometimes it swims in great circles, creating an almighty wake; other times, it lashes the surface with its tail or leaps clear of the water, to come crashing back down in a storm of violent waves capable of washing a surfer all the way to the shore!

Every member of the WVWF has had a few turns already. Yeti is probably the most capable surfer, although Billy Psycho is also very skilled. Metal Ed doesn't appear to know what is going on, but seems to enjoy being hurled around by the water.

Captain Awesome is something else altogether. Perched on his board, surfing troos pulled up to his nipples, he almost appears to be meditating whilst he surfs; gently moving his weight around when necessary and often smoking his Vewdu Pipe! I've been watching all day and I don't think I've seen him fall off even once! Perhaps this is where he got his name...

Thus far, there have been no fatalities.

LOG ENTRY: THIRTY-FIVE
A Surfing Lesson

Inevitably, Captain Awesome eventually sought me out and handed me a Vewdu Board. I explained to him that I have never ridden a way before: not in the sea, not in a lake and certainly never in the wake of a Sharktopus.

That didn't seem to bother him. He simply sketched the outline of a board on the floor and made me practise lying down on it on my stomach, then leaping back up again. Apparently this will help.

I held my tongue regarding the absence of waves on the land (and the absence of a Sharktopus). There are only so many protestations a Guildsman can make before he simply gives up and embraces his fate.

If I die, know that I always said surfing was a stupid pastime.

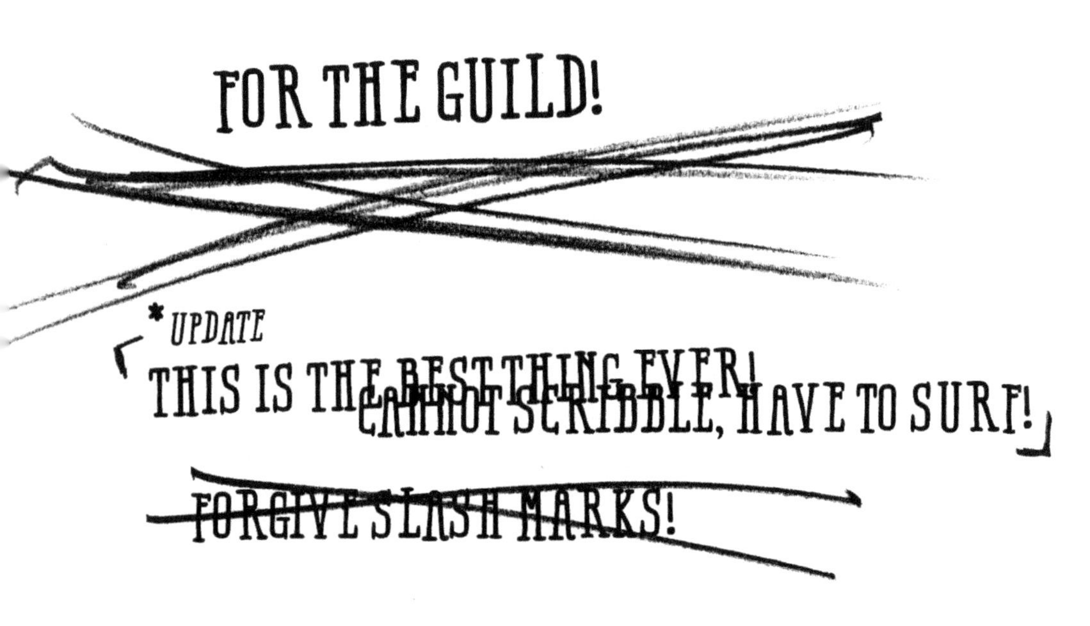

LOG ENTRY: THIRTY-SIX
The Wave

Surfing is my destiny.
I was born for this. I shall rename myself...Wave Catcher.

No, Wave Rider!
No, Storm Turtle!

I'll come up with a name later.

Maybe I don't even need a name: I'll just become one with the water. When people talk about the wave, they'll be talking about me.

...and by 'me'...I mean 'the wave'.

Can't continue scribbling: the wave is calling me back again.
I mean, I am calling me back again.
I mean, I am calling the wave...the...

Never mind.

LOG ENTRY: THIRTY-SEVEN
Midnight Surf

Everybody has gone to bed.

Everybody... except The Wave.

The Wave does not sleep.

The Wave simply... is.

The Sharktopus is still active.

THE WAVE
~~I~~ could have one more ride.

One more – alone on the lake.

Then The Wave will sleep.

Maybe.

VB

OOHHHHHH!!!

LOG ENTRY: THIRTY-EIGHT

Based on my scattered fragments of memory, I believe I was ripped over the side of the lake by some kind of colossal waterfall. I must have been concentrating too hard on not falling into the water to notice it. The irony is not lost on me, even here...wherever I am.

I vaguely recall tumbling beard-over-boots in a plunge-pool for some time. Although – alas – I was not actually wearing my boots! I had taken them off to surf and now we are apart, perhaps forever...

Eventually, I was unceremoniously spat out and sucked into some kind of underground river-tunnel system. I have been bobbing along on my board ever since.

I am alone. Alone in the darkness. How long I have been here is a mystery, for there is neither day nor night. There is only blackness: inky, crushing, blackness. I imagine this is similar to the experience of wearing a cake on your head, except much less delicious.

This, I accept, depends on the cake.

I have managed to set fire to the only dry object I can find (my hat) to provide me with some warmth and shed enough light to enscribble my log. If I don't make it out of here alive, at least my adventures will live on.

Thus, the Guild.

Alone

The hat is burning surprisingly well. It has been kept bone dry by my meta-hat, in a miracle of Guild engineering. Perhaps years of sweat have built up around the inside to create a limitless store of fuel for the fire. This is a thought too disgusting to consider for long.

The last thing I remember clearly is riding the swell of the Sharktopus' wake. I remember it was midnight and the moon was high: shining bright and silver on the lake, whilst the WYWF slept in the bunk house.

Why was I out surfing on my own in the middle of the night?

I don't even like surfing! Do I?

On the plus side, nothing is trying to eat me. Yet.

All I have left, apart from my board and clothes, is this log book (which never leaves my side), my hat and meta-hat, and a length of clambering twine that I had wrapped around myself. (*I was planning on using it as a rescue device if I tumbled off my board and wound up floundering in the lake*).

For now, I must conserve my source of light and warmth. I shall extinguish the hat. I'm not sure which will become unbearable first: the cold or the dark.

I am trying to scribble without lighting the hat.

It seems to be going well.

I must be even more powerful a chronicler than I realised!

THINGS I DO BETTER IN THE DARK

M o u r n

Paint and/or decorate

Dance: also works well in the moonlight

Play dice: I am luckier when I can't see

B A K E

THE HIGH JUMP

When I escape this underground realm, perhaps I shall scribble my log with my eyes closed.

I shall be called The Sightless Scholar.

Ol' Eyeless. Blinderson.

I won't actually be blind, of course. It will be a...

gimmick.

LOG ENTRY: THIRTY-NINE
Scribbling in the Dark

LOG ENTRY: FORTY
A Mistake

I was hasty in my decision to attempt enscribblment in the dark.

I lit the hat, just to check on my progress.

How embarrassing.

In future, I shall only scribble with ample light.

LOG ENTRY: FORTY-ONE Noises in the Dar

It is no good. I have had to light the hat again. It wasn't the dark or the cold that got to me in the end. It was the noises!

I must have fallen asleep: one moment there was nothing but the gurgle of the river and in the next thing I knew the air was abuzz (*or rather, aroar*) with sounds.

Terrifying sounds!

I am trying to remember everything I have learned about the less-hospitable creatures of this island. Those that live in the Thundra on the other side of the Twisted Peaks.

What were they? Bearhawks: the mythical and terrifying half bear, half hawk. Nothmen: half men, half...well, moth presumably. That sounds a lot less intimidating than the Bearhawk.

What else? Gnomen? Warebits? Napes - those were meant to be pretty mighty? Sirens? Fuzz...ez?

It's no use. I know nothing that could help me fight off a Nape, let alone a Bearhawk.

Only one thing is for certain. The noises are getting louder.

For now, I shall extinguish the hat.

But I shall keep my punching-fist clenched.

The beasts! These...monsters!

I cannot see them through the darkness, but I hear them calling me onwards!

No. No, I **feel** them calling me onwards!

LOG ENTRY: FORTY-TWO
NO ESCAPE

They – whatever they may be – are pulling me in; dragging me down, down this ... stream?

There can be no escape.

Blackness. Nothing but blackness. Blackness and eyes. Glowing eyes. In the blackness.

EYES?!

LOG ENTRY: FORTY-THREE A LOW

TO WAR, TO WAR!

Thunder and fists have met in the dark: FOR THE GUILD!

The extent of my wounds remains a mystery.

Silence now.

There are no wounds. Were there ever any?

Were there even any eyes?

I shall rest.

The hunger many be the death of me.
I have not breakfeasted in...
By the Nine Big Faces of the Guild:
I cannot even remember my
last breakfeast!
No Guildsman should perish
in such a state.
I have disgraced myself.

Has it come to this?
Must I literally eat my own hat?
Perhaps there is sustenance somewhere
in its oily folds.
My eyes have adapted to the gloom.
I am as a bat.
No, wait.

A cat.

I awoke today to discover I had no feet. Fortunately, I found them again before the panic set in. They were hidden in my boots. I will not be so quick to trust them in the future.

Note to self: never put hat in mouth again.

I have just remembered I lost my boots some time ago.
Where were my feet hiding?!

LOG ENTRY: F
A Friend

I made a friend today. He is a fine fellow and, although he is much shorter than Yeti, he too is covered in hair! Perhaps they are kin.

By all accounts (*there is no evidence to the contrary*) he is a talented bladesman, like myself. He also hasn't suggested that he lacks vigour in a foot race or would hold back in a good old fashioned bellowing contest.

He doesn't eat much, but then again neither do I at the moment, on account of being hopelessly lost on an underground river with neither food nor... food, in sight.

He hasn't told me his name so I have taken to calling him Archibald, after my mother. She loved that name. I think. She never said that she hated it, that's for sure.

Archibald's hobbies include juggling and tossing the caber. He holds a formal qualification in vegetables and is a three-time three-legged race champion.

He is also a coconut.

I have never been friends with a coconut before.

I shall speak softly, in case his hearing is extra sensitive. I don't know why it would be, but then again I don't know anything about coconuts at all.

Except that their husks are excellent for stuffing mattresses.

I shall try not to mention that in conversation.

LOG ENTRY: FORTY-FIVE
Back To Normal

It is good to have some company. Reading back through my journal entries by hat-light, I worry that the starvation and solitude have been affecting me recently.

Now that I am back in my right mind, I am half-tempted to rip out the offending pages and cast them into the murky depths!

I shall not. They must live on as a reminder of those tough times.

I cannot scribble any more at the moment, Archibald is waiting. We have a lunchtime booking at Riche Riche Restaurant and I have misplaced my bow-tie.

I have looked everywhere: under my hat, on the surfboard, in my pockets, under my hat, on the surfboard, under my hat – it's nowhere to be found!

I shall be the ugliest belle at the ugly ball.

Yet again.

Hams Sally shall mock me upon my return.

I have found my bow-tie. It was under my hat.

LOG ENTRY: FORTY-SIX

Dreams

Archibald and I are getting along just fine.

We start what might be the day by describing our dreams from what we assume was the night before. We interpret them for one another. I tend to just make up any old nonsense, but Archibald is very insightful.

The other night, I dreamed that I was falling. Archibald said it was because I feel "out of control" of some element of my daily life. How could he know such a thing?!

In what might be the afternoon, I lash the clambering twine around my waist, attach the other end to the board and go for a leisurely swim in the pitch black water. I am secretly trying to find land or catch fish. I don't tell Archibald: nothing is crueler than false hope.

Come what could be the evening, we swap tales and sing songs, until the constant darkness gets the best of us and we drift into a peaceful slumber.

It is not a bad life.

RECENT DREAM INTERPRETATIONS

I am being chased on horseback by Duncan Von Socks. We enter a race. At the final hurdle, my horse becomes an aged cow.

↳ ***I have made some bad decisions, recently.***

I jump from a window above a river and land in a floating casino. I gamble and lose my eyebrows. Everybody laughs. I do not laugh.

↙ ***I am not expressing my emotions properly these days.***

I hire a squirrel assassin. He arrives in a bucket. The shock kills him. I bury him at sea.

I am long overdue a holiday.

CHOP!

I attempt to jump over my own head, but my knees have been replaced by lungs. I cannot breathe.

I have taken on too much responsibility and yearn for the freedom to stretch myself, creatively.

I am packed into a small bag and put into an empty bathing tub, which is then filled with semi-precious beans.

I am worried that my burdens have caused me to miss out on good opportunities.

Over the course of a day, a small rock rolls slowly down a hillock. A seagull watches and weeps. Am I the rock? Or the hillock? Or the tears?

I fear my punching fist will make a violent bid for its freedom.

Two cats dance until they became a single large cigar. An old man wants to smoke the cigar, but his arms are too long. The cigar lights itself. The smoke forms what could be the letter J.

The people I thought were my parents are actually my children.

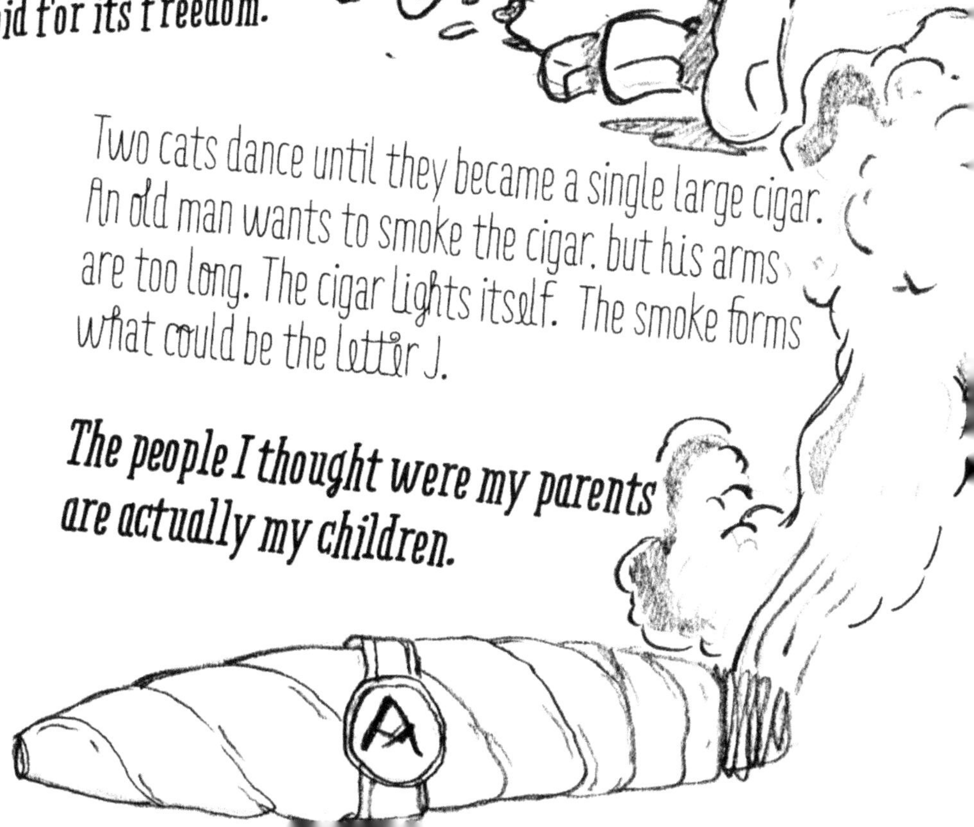

ODE TO A BISCUIT

O gather ye 'round for a tale I shall tell,
Of a cracker as bold as he was handsome, as well.
By the name Sir Charles Biscuit he was cleverly called,
And he journeyed the world, whilst in a pocket installed.

Oh the danger it grew as the farther he travelled,
As around him the fibres of trousers unravelled.
All family consumed, each one of them eaten,
His courage ne'er faltered, his resolve ne'er was beaten.

One day a hand, good for punching no doubt,
Snatched up Sir Charles and hoisted him out.
"What have we here?" bellow its beard,
"An oat cracker not damaged, nor even a-feared?"

The handsome McCuba, a man of great fame,
Saved Sir Charles biscuit and gave him a name.
Then, as best friends, they endured water and cold,
With their comrade the coconut, named Archibald.

LOG ENTRY: FORTY-SEVEN
Ejection

I was ejected from my underground realm sometime tonight.

One minute I was floating along minding my own business. If I remember correctly, I was composing a ballad about the tenacious Sir Charles Biscuit: an oat cracker I found tucked away in the recesses of my trousers. How he survived this long is a mystery and an inspiration.

I was so lost in the creative process that I didn't notice the roaring, or my board picking up speed. The next thing I knew, I was plummeting into some kind of...vortex! By the time I had gathered the wits and breath to utter my famous last words: "TO ALL A GOOD NIGHT!" I plunged beard-first into a churning maelstrom of pitch black water.

My board must have popped out of the water seconds later. For me, however, surfacing was a struggle. We Guildsmen are strong swimmers, but we are not usually laden down with robes, hats, ropes and so on.

Combined with the dead weight of my sodden beard, I feared I would never make it to the surface.

When I did, it was more than I could manage to stay afloat. As my limbs turned numb, I felt myself start to sink. Luckily, just as I dipped below the surface of the water, my board floated by within seizing distance. With one last massive exertion, I grabbed hold of it and kicked my way to shore with all the strength I could muster from my once-mighty quadriceps.

Archibald made it to safety first; he is a strong swimmer. The same cannot be said for Sir Charles Biscuit. He has become...en-soggied. Perhaps fatally.

Luckily, I keep my log book in the oiled and waterproof folds of my Guild robes. Otherwise I would be without any Book of Deeds whatsoever – and then what?

We have made camp for the night, but I cannot rest easy.

I must secure the perimeters.

I have established a perimeter around us. I shall take the first watch. None shall pass.

All is quiet on the perimeter front.

But what of the back?

All is quiet on the back, too.

BUT NOW WHAT OF THE FRONT!

Still quiet on the front.

BUT WHAT OF THE BACK?!

The back is still fine, but I'm not sure how much longer I can keep this up. Archibald is doing his best, but he is simply not equipped for the task at hand. He has no hands, for one thing.

Perhaps some rum will soothe my troubled mind and put some steel back in my belly...

I must take care to sip it; I don't know how long we will be here and I must make it last.

I have drunk all the rum. All hope is lost.

THE STRANGER SMILES UPON ME: I HAVE FOUND A FRESH BOTTLE OF RUM!

I shall open it immediately.

This is not rum. This is my boot.

How I cracked it open is a mystery.

When will dawn come?

I'm not sure how long I can make this boot last.

I must maintain.

So tired. Need sleep-rest. A tired Guildsman is a forgetful Guildsman, and a forgetful Guildsman is a forgetful Guildsman and he, whomsoever forgets, is a Guildsman...not... So tired. Must rest. A tired Guildsman is a forgetful... Where was I?

It is Archibald's turn to take the watch, but I don't like to wake him – he looks so peaceful.

My hat shall take the next watch instead.

Be vigilant, sir.

YE GADS! I HAVE LOST AN ARM IN MY SLUMBER! THE BEASTS INTEND TO DEVOUR ME PIECE BY PIECE!

I blame the watchman.

NEVER TRUST A HAT!

False alarm: I merely slept awkwardly.

The feeling has now returned to my arm. For a while it was like a having a cold, dead turkey dangling from my body.

(A burly turkey, if I say so myself. Which I do.)

I must remember to apologise to my hat.

I believe I may have struck it in my anger.

EMERGENCY: THERE IS A MAN TRAPPED BELOW THE WATER!

STOP SCRIBBLING, MAN: HE MUST BE SAVED!

Archibald has admitted he is too afraid to take the plunge.

I dare not ask my hat after insulting it earlier.

So be it. I shall don the Face of the Wrestler and steel my courage!

If I drown in the process of rescuing this poor soul, remember me as man of wit and dense musculature.

TO ALL A GOODNIGHT!

The man in the pool was me. I wasn't drowning: I was a reflection.

I should trim my beard.

And come up with some new last words.

We buried the remains of Sir Charles Biscuit beneath a cluster of pebbles. He would have liked it there. Possibly. In honesty,

I never really knew him.

There is an awkward silence developing between me and my hat.

Daybreak cannot come soon enough.

C. BISCUIT

LOG ENTRY: FORTY-EIGHT Dawn

Dawn. Beautiful dawn! Even as I scribble these words is breaking all around me, the strange golden glow illuminating my position and shedding some light (*literally*) on last night's events.

A few ship's lengths from my current position (*a muddy bank*) there is a large crag which sports twin holes in its side, much like eyes. From each eye, a waterfall gushes into the foaming sea – giving the impression that the rock face is weeping.

I shall name it...the Crying Cliff. I have no idea which of these waterfalls spat me out, but I am grateful to it for doing so. I salute you, Crying Cliff. Long may your torment linger, if you'll pardon the expression.

This is the first daylight I have seen since I was swept from the lake and I can already feel the mania of my subterranean incarceration fading. It is strange what happens to the mind when left alone in the dark for so long.

Still, I'm back to my sensible old self now. That said, I do have some bad news...but I also have some good news and some more good news. Which would you like first?

THE GOOD NEWS

My hat has forgiven me for falsely accusing it of inattentiveness.
It understands the burden of leadership weighs heavily upon my beard.
We embraced and I offered it a retribution punch, which it politely denied.
I am lucky to have found companionship in such dark times.

THE BAD NEWS

Judging by my surroundings, I have popped out on the 'other side' of the island. The Thundra, as they call it – or they would call it, if they ever spoke about. Specifically, I believe I am in the Yewdu Woods.

There is a touch of malice about the whole place. Everything is... edgier. Spiker, even. The trees, for example, are angular and almost seem to scowl at me.

The ground seems more hostile, too. It is rougher, rockier and (*where it isn't unpleasantly dry*) it is alarmingly damp and sticky. I don't want to stay still for too long, which is just as well because I get the feeling that, if I did, I would become stuck.

The noise is constant. A ceaseless dull roaring and screaming, like a hundred waterfalls watching some kind of waterfall-based team sport. Plungeball?

My presence here will almost certainly not go unnoticed by whatever is lurking here. I assume something is lurking...

Yeah, something will be lurking.

THE MORE GOOD NEWS

As the sun rises and the morning mists clear, I can see a beach far in the distance. I would have to swim a long way around the rocky outcrops of the Twisted Peaks to get to it, but it appears to be back on the civilised side of the island.

Archibald is looking well-rested. This is just as well, for we have a long and gruelling journey ahead of us. We start after breakfeast.

UNEXPECTED EXTRA BAD NEWS!

There is no breakfeast. We begin immediately!
Moisten the wenches: we are heading home!

FOR THE GUILD!

TO ALL A GOODNIGHT!

?..
SAVIOR COVE
?

LOG ENTRY: FORTY-NINE
Adrift

We are adrift.

Sometime after daybreak, Archibald and I launched our surfboard into the waves and struck out for the beach. We made good progress; Archibald says I am stronger in the arm than any man he has met before. I have promised to introduce him to Quaffer Harris once I am back in the Guild Hall.

Soon the roaring and madness was far behind us and the golden beach of freedom was visibly drawing closer.

Eventually, I could hear the roaring no more. We were safe.

It was at this moment that I started having second thoughts. This is bad news for a Guildsman: we rarely have first thoughts, let alone seconds!

Nevertheless, we must continue. Forgive me if my entries into this log become less frequent. I must concentrate on paddling if we are ever to make the distant shores.

UPDATE

By the Nine Faces, the sun is cooking me alive! I have pulled the brims of my hat down as far as they will go, but it is little use.

Poor Archibald is being fried like a hairy egg. He hasn't complained even once, however. Truly, he is a stoic fellow.

In desperation I am paddling for the shore, but we don't seem to be making any progress. Maybe this undertaking was too great, even for us...

I fear my hat has perished. It hasn't uttered a word since we set out.

UPDATE

My arms are like lead: LETHAL! Yet also heavy. So heavy. Forgive my scrawl; I can barely even scribble down this entry.

The beach is so close, but I haven't the energy to paddle another inch. Yet I must. One stroke more. Then another. Count to ten between each one. The beach is ours for the conquering.

---

t's no use, I am done. I can go no farther. I am marooned on y surfboard with only Archibald to witness my demise. ven he cannot manage a single stroke more.

He is a coconut, after all.

Perhaps the tide will wash us our bodies ashore...

Perhaps.

MC

LOG ENTRY: FIFTY
The Dream

He came to me in a dream.

I only closed my eyes for a moment and there he was: eyes burning like unattended bacon beneath the grill of inquisition; beefy arms crossed across a beefier chest; unfathomably dense beard rigid despite the billowing sea winds.

The Guildmaster himself...apparently walking on the water.

He didn't say anything. He didn't have to. His presence alone spoke volumes: he would never lie down mid-deed and let the sun bake him like a potato.

I am no potato. I am a man. A man of the Guild! A GUILDSMAN!

[AND I LITERALLY DO NOT UNDERSTAND THE MEANING OF THE WORD DEFEAT! (*I think it's like victory, only...slower?*)]

At that moment, the Guildmaster disappeared and something heavy fell out of my hat. It rolled onto the surfboard and collided with Archibald. Before the sea could pitch and toss it overboard, I reached out and snatched it up. It felt familiar in my grasp...

MC

I snapped it open and gazed upon the dials. For the first time ever, they were both pointing the exact same direction: backwards. Back towards the Thundra.

No sign could be any clearer. Glory – and rum – lay back from whence I came. I must return.

Yet if I never make it back, who will sing of my deeds? Will I never again raise the mighty Horn of Adventure and Rebirth beneath the Full Moon? Will my deeds amount to nothing? Is there glory in perishing upon the open sea, in a vague attempt to seek out adventure and rum?

Irrelevant. Better to die a Guildsman than live as a...whatever other people are. Muggles?

I RETURN!

FOR THE GUILD!

And also for the rum.

Mainly for the rum.

UPDATE

Although I have realised I am not destined to perish on this curiously-coloured ocean, I can't help but feel I'd benefit from some sustenance: a horn of mead, a braised ox or an entire flock of geese...

That said, I'm in the middle of the sea: it's probably full of edible things. I'm sure I can spear me a fish, punch me a shark or scoop me up some general floating nutrients.

Why, there is a coconut bobbing right alongside my surfboard already – that'll make a good starter!

I have made a terrible mistake.

I cannot scribble much, I must tend to my companion. I have set up my hat as a makeshift bed and crafted bandages from strips of my shirt.

By the Faces, Codename McCuba: what hast thou dons't?

I hear coconut water can be used to replace human blood in a transfusion. Does it work the other way around, I wonder?

Part of me hopes not...

As far as I can tell, Archibald's condition has stabilised. He is sleeping peacefully. I think he's going to make it.

I cannot believe I forgot about him. It shall never happen again!

Can coconuts wake up?

WAS ARCHIBALD EVER AWAKE?

Has any coconut ever been truly awake?

AM I TRULY AWAKE?

How can I be sure this isn't some kind of awful rum-dream?

Such are my meditations.

LOG ENTRY: FIFTY-ONE Genius

If I say so myself (*which I regularly do*), I am a genius. Blessed as we have been by this gale, I have managed to rig my pantaloons as a kind of sail. It is not the most effective set-up and it requires me to lie on my back with my legs in the air, but we are making steady progress.

Archibald's wounds have not dampened his spirit. Incredibly, he bears no grudge: he says he would have done the same in my position. I must bear this in mind in the coming days.

He disagrees about the sail situation, however. He questions the point in our survival if we destroy our pride in the process.

He has much to learn about the Guild.

I can hear the roaring again. This time it sounds like a challenge.

LOG ENTRY: FIFTY-TWO
Progress

We make good progress. Indeed, I am singing the Progress Song. It goes thus:

PROGRESS – PROGRESS,
WE, WE PROGRESS.
LIKE THE WOLF ACROSS THE PLAIN,
WE, WE PROGRESS.

YONDER – YONDER,
WE, WE PROGRESS.
LIKE THE BEAR ACROSS THE PLAIN,
WE, WE PROGRESS.

FARTHER – FARTHER,
WE, WE PROGRESS.
LIKE THE OX ACROSS THE PLAIN,
WE, WE PROGRESS.

STRONGER – STRONGER
WE, WE PROGRESS.
LIKE THE AARDVARK ACRO...

Archibald has just snapped at me. He says I should do more progressing and less journal-enscribblment.

He has a point.

I really like the Progress Song, though. I'll finish it later.

LOG ENTRY: FIFTY-THREE: LAND!

Land!

It is...ho?

Made it. Beach. Too tired. Limbs like hemp.

Thank the Poet for the Progress Song.
It was our saviour.

Archibald disagrees. He says it is a bad song and that I should be ashamed.

I shall fight him in the morn.

ROOAAAAR!!

LOG ENTRY: FIFTY-FOUR
I Am The Hunter

During the night, I was rudely shaken from my exhausted slumber by a deafening roar. As a man who knows his roars, I immediately identified it as a large beastie, with...teeth and...possibly wings. Or perhaps no wings, but...udders. Or...knees.

I should have paid more attention in Hunting Class. Alas, I was always too busy – HUNTING! Badly, I now realise. Ah well.

When I had regained my balance (*both physically and spiritually*), I set out to find the source of the noise. I am knowledgeable enough about roars to know that whatever made the noise was probably about the size of the surrounding trees, so I shinned my way up one and peered out into the darkness.

Nothing stirred. The night was calm. Tediously calm. I even considered calling out a challenge, or at least bearing my chest to the starry sky, just to make the climb worthwhile.

Suddenly, before I could rip off my shirt, there was an eruption of flame: the air itself seemed to be ablaze and filled with the unmistakable stench of cooking flesh!

Naturally, I dived for cover. In my panic, however, I forgot that I was atop a mighty tree. The fall would have killed a lesser man. Luckily for me, a Guildsman always lands on his feet. I mean his beard. A Guildsman always lands on his beard...

Somehow (*through years of training, I suppose*) I managed to turn my landing in to graceful roll. Then I leapt – like a muscular salmon – into a nearby pool. There, in a feat of creative genius, I re-purposed my Vewdu pipe as a makeshift snorkel-scope to ensure I stayed submerged for the duration of the inferno.

Whilst down there, I took some time to reflect on my situation. I concluded, once again, that I need to find a way off this island.

Eventually, the burning subsided and I emerged – dripping and somewhat shrivelled, I imagine – into the darkness.

Come sunrise, I shall find the cause of this mayhem. And we shall have words.

Stern words.

OWNER CARVED MARK!

Pot made from the Seed of a Jufu berry

The Shaft dark straw Veridu spruce wood

BONE smooth tip

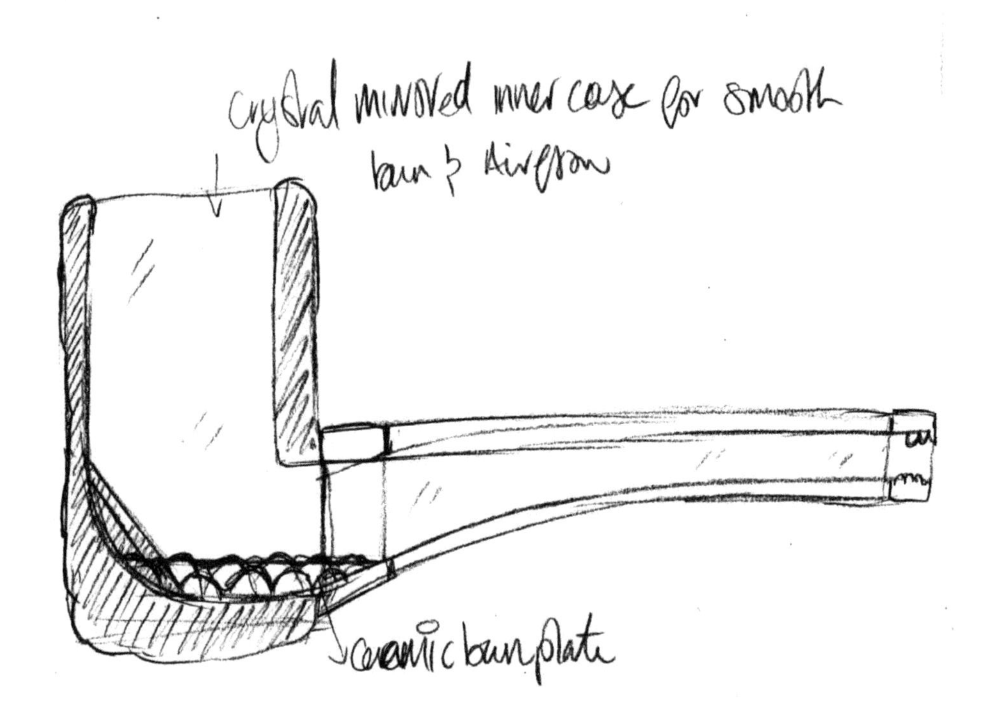

I rose early this morning and breakfeasted on berries and nuts. It was not a pleasant experience.

I performed my squats, had a bit of a bellow, combed my beard with a handful of twigs and armed myself with a gnarled branch. I sharpened one end into a deadly point and carved some Power Runes into the shaft. Thus equipped, I meditated on the task at hand.

It didn't take long. After all, I know nothing of the task at hand. I shall stroll around until I find the beast. Then I shall slay it, using whichever technique first comes to find – plus this sharpened stick.

'Tis a real quest. Fraught with danger, uncertainty and makeshift weaponry. Once it is complete, I shall parade around with some kind of trophy until somebody showers me with riches. Then I shall shower. Money makes me feel dirty. As do quests.

I shall be like the Guildsmen of Old: The Rum Monks. Perhaps I should braid herbs into my beard. I feel like the Rum Monks would have done that. I don't know why.

Archibald has plaited his hair into war-braids. He has also painted his face with his family colours. Combined with his horrific head wounds, he makes quite the fearsome sight.

Now, I suppose, the time has come for battle.

If I do not return, know that I died in combat – like my mother. Remember me as a Scholar of the Great Adventure.

(Also, please also feed Archibald. He may go into mourning.)

LOG ENTRY: FIFTY-FIVE
Reximus

I have had a very curious day.

Oh, forgive me, I should have mentioned: I am alive. I could have startled you or...something.

Having worked myself up into a full blown Rum Frenzy – ready for war – I charged the area in which I believed my enemy was lying in wait.

And guess what. There it was! Frankly the sheer surprise of being correct was enough to knock me off my feet. Luckily I had Archibald to stabilise myself, as I gazed across the clearing to our opponent.

It was everything I had feared, although admittedly with fewer udders. It was a towering, fire-spouting colossus of a monster: reptilian in appearance, yet covered in dense matted hair. Like a dragon wearing an old fur coat.

I must admit I started wondering about my decision to go to war. Alas, the Guild forbids regret. Thus, we made our advance.

Upon catching sight of us, the monster bellowed with rage. Dropping to all fours, it lumbered forth for the kill. By this point, even the ever-stalwart Archibald was showing visible signs of concern. (*Let the records show that he didn't falter for a second.*)

With the beast came the smell. The stench of burning flesh! The reek of seared meat! The oddly familiar stink of cooking skin!

It was unmistakable...

ZILLA

Then the beast was upon us. I swung my club up to protect my face and adopted Stance of the Wrestler. Legs wide; arms wide; beard wide. Stable, like a...horse's house.

Apparently surprised by my unwavering courage, the monster skidded to a halt and lashed out with wickedly sharp talons. From each claw dangled a huge sack of meat. Mouth agape to reveal hundreds of twisted teeth, it roared in my face a sound like this:

"THAU-THAGE!"

Club aloft, I froze. What trickery was this? Some kind of battle challenge? A call to arms? Was it mocking me? Why wasn't it trying to devour me, boots n' all? (*That is purely a turn of phrase: my boots are long gone - and I still feel the sting of their absence. Especially when I step on Archibald*).

"Thau-thage?"

Mega Sausage!

It bellowed again, quieter this time – almost questioningly. It waved it claws in front of me, the sacks of meat swinging in front of my face. I was struck dumb with confusion. The beast seemed to sigh. Then, clearly, it spoke:

"*Would...you...like...a...thauthage?*"

At last, the penny dropped. The monster was talking. And it had a lisp. These sacks of meat were giant sausages. That was the smell.

I wasn't sure what to say. The Rum Frenzy was still pumping in my ears. Luckily, my stomach answered for me with a growl...

The beast grinned, terrifyingly, and dumped a mega-sausage down in front of me.

"*Tuck in!*" he invited us, gleefully; "*They're thimply the betht!*"

Thus I met Reximus, the lisping barbecusaurus.

LOG ENTRY: FIFTY-SIX
Sausages and Secrets

This sausage is taking some getting through. It is bigger than my kicking leg, for one thing. For another, it does not taste like any animal I have ever encountered. I don't know why this surprises me.

Even so, it certainly isn't unpleasant and it is the first decent thing I have eaten since my hangover breakfeast (*with the exception of Archibald's brains, but we have vowed never to mention that again*).

"There'th nothing like cooking with flameth!" Reximus crooned with satisfaction when he noticed the gusto with which I went about devouring the meat. He is a curious fellow. There isn't an aggressive body in his body.

He spends most the day lazing around on the ground, humming to himself and cramming minced-up somethingorother into sheaths to form long tubes. At every sausage-sized interval along the tube, he makes a gap in the mince and twists the sheath to form long chains of sausage-shaped...sausages. These he piles into a large mound, for storage.

When his hunger finally gets the better of him, Reximus leaps into the mound of tubes in a frenzy of claws. He skewers half a dozen mega-sausages onto some kind of makeshift lance, then draws himself up to his full and horrifying size, raises the sausages to mouth-level and blows great gouts of flames over them, flame-grilling them to perfection with practised ease...

...and burning his tongue quite badly in the process.

In a curious twist of evolution, Reximus' mouth isn't quite fireproof.

"Motht people thuthpect the lithp ith a thpeech impediment – but it ithn't tho! It ith thimply a downthide to breathing flameth."

"It'th a curth" he sobbed in a particularly painful moment, great tears the size of pineapples falling from his eyes. "It getth tho thore!
But it'th the only way to cook the thauthages."

There is something quite poetic about his plight. Perhaps I shall scribble myself an opera about it when I get home.

My curiosity finally got the better of me today and I summoned the courage to ask Reximus what goes into his sausages.

"THECRETH!"

he declared defensively, narrowing his eyes and glancing all around him.

I started to ask whether he would at least tell me the primary form of meat, but he leapt into the air bellowing:

"QUIET QUIET!"

Then suddenly, he lowered himself to my level and whispered:
"There could be a thpy hiding in the treeth..."

I left it at that.

LOG ENTRY: FIFTY-SEVEN
En-Strengthening

Forgive my lack of entries; it has been some time since my last.

I have been busy: en-strengthening myself!!

I still don't know what these sausages are made of, but I gorge myself daily on their sustenance.

Weakened after their recent inactivity, my legs are finally starting to regain their old strength.

It will take a while before I am at my full physical prowess again, however. In my current state, I am not sure I could leap a charging moose – the minimum requirement for a man of the Guild. I could probably manage a caribou.

5 THINGS I COULD CURRENTLY LEAP

1. SWAN
2. BARREL OF ALE
3. AVERAGE-SIZED FERN
4. MOST CHAIRS
5. TWO GOATS

LOG ENTRY: FIFTY-EIGHT
Departure

The time has come for me to leave Reximus. I came back here for adventures, not sausages. Reximus doesn't understand the difference.

Bless him.

He has agreed to help me, nevertheless. He has told me of an old lighthouse keeper, who – like me – became marooned on this island, some time back. From the top of his lighthouse, I should be able to look out over the whole island.

This sounds like a good place to start!

I haven't known him long, but I have forged a close friendship with Reximus. He has assured me that if I ever need his assistance, I must simply spark up a barbecue and use the smoke to draw the shape of a sausage in the sky. He will come running.

Honestly, I don't know if that is any use to me. Still, it is the thought that counts.

Reximus has also given me a farewell sausage, which I shall carry across my shoulders like a maiden in distress. I'm not sure which I would prefer it was at the moment.

On the one hand, I do need some kind of fuel to make it through the Thundra.

On the other hand, I do like maidens.

Especially when they are distressed.

LOG ENTRY: FIFTY-NINE
To the Lighthouse

I am happy with the sausage situation. Food must come first. Especially right now: lunch time.

I am making decent progress. I think. I'm moving swiftly, but everything looks so similar that I cannot actually tell how far I have travelled.

I must finish eating and get moving. I feel as though I'm sinking into the ground!

Night has fallen and with it the desire for a maiden has grown. I have found some solid ground to sleep upon.

I woke up this morning spooning the sausage.

Do not ask me why I feel the need to document this fact.

Perhaps it is the loneliness and isolation. Perhaps it is the overwhelming sense that I am totally lost.

I find myself clinging to any solid truth.

No matter how embarrassing.

LOG ENTRY: SIXTY-ONE
First Glimpse

Tonight I caught my first glimpse of what must be the illumination from the lighthouse, blinking solemnly in the dark distance.

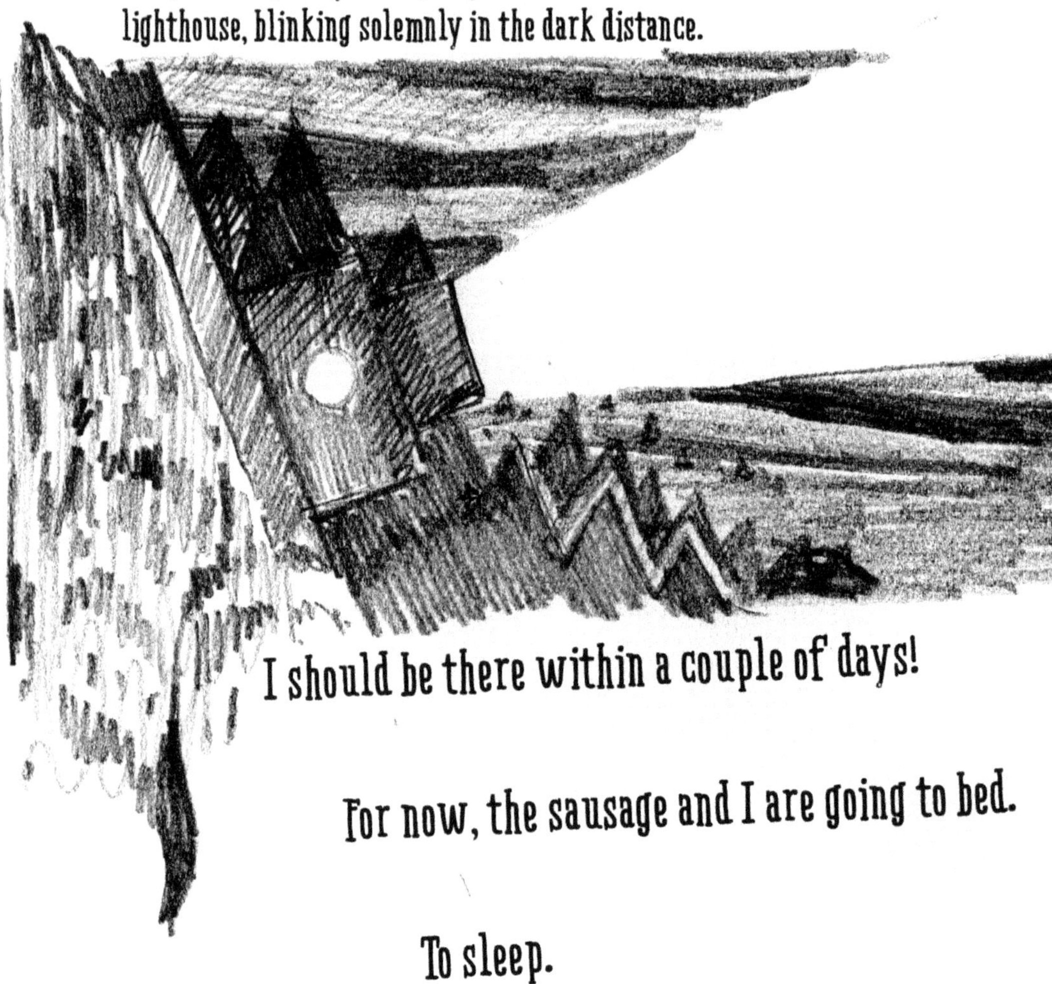

I should be there within a couple of days!

For now, the sausage and I are going to bed.

To sleep.

LOG ENTRY: SIXTY-TWO

No Progress.

It has been at least a week since my last entry.

I simply cannot bring myself to enscribble.

I am not making any progress.

I storm onwards every day: at Guild pace, no less. Every time I have a meal, my burden grows lighter – and I move all the quicker. By all accounts I should have made it to the lighthouse days ago.

Yet when night falls, the blinking light is as far away as ever.

I know not where I am, or which way to go.
I know not even which way is back.

I have the unshakable feeling that I am covering the same ground over and over again.

I shall start marking every tree I pass with my personal rune, just to be sure.

In good news, I have solved the sausage/maiden dilemma.

Why can it not be both?

I have named her Roxana, after my grandfather.

LOG ENTRY: SIXTY-THREE
A Good Sign?

I have still not passed any marked trees yet, so I must be progressing in some direction or another.

This is good news!

Potentially.

LOG ENTRY: SIXTY-FOUR
Marked Tree

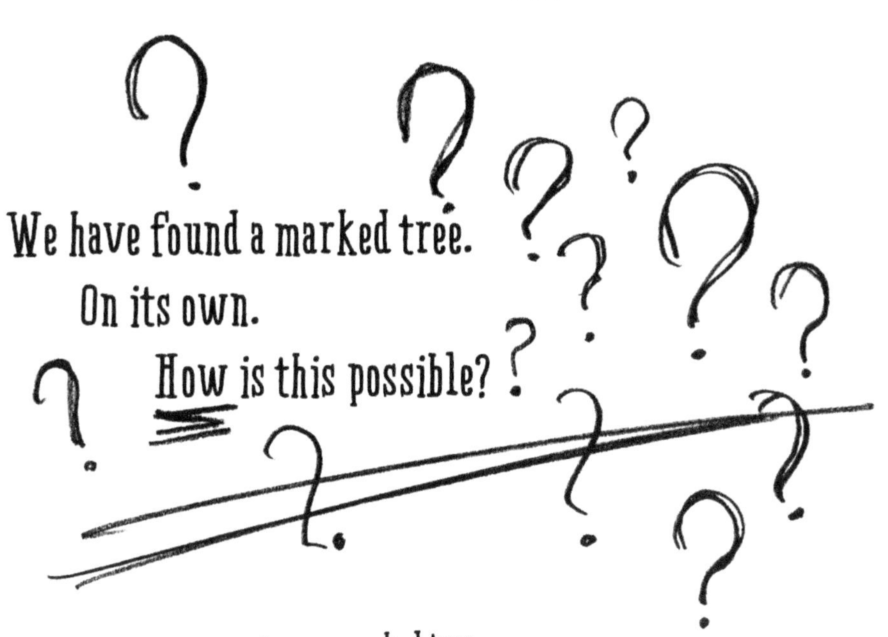

Another solitary marked tree.

Perhaps it is me.

Maybe I am failing to do...something...

The confusion is overwhelming.

Thank the Big Faces that I have Roxana to comfort me.

The quickest way to a Guildsman's heart is through his belly.

(The ceaseless feasting means our organs get quite severly restructured.)

LOG ENTRY: SIXTY-FIVE
Crazy?

This is going to sound crazy.
I think the trees are moving.
Scurrying, even.

They never do it when I'm watching.
They are too savvy for that.

I have asked Roxana to keep watch.
I trust her.

She is delicious, after all.

LOG ENTRY: SIXTY-SIX

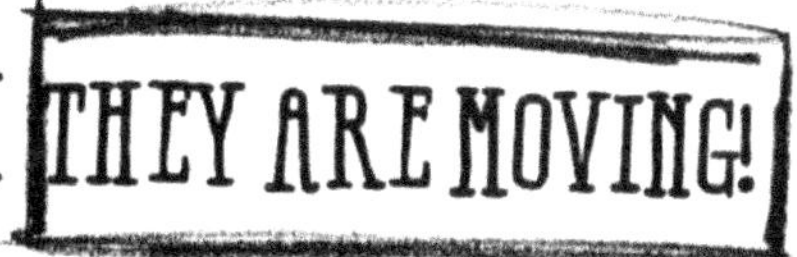

THEY ARE MOVING!!!

I HAVE SEEN IT WITH MY OWN EYES!

Roxana saw it too, so I know I'm not going crazy.

It was around dusk. I had just finished my dinner and stretched out on the floor to sleep.

Suddenly, out of the corner of my eye, I spied movement!

As soon as I turned to look, all was still.

I lay back. This time, I draped my beard over my face and watched through the hairs.

Sure enough, when it thought I wasn't looking, one of the trees hoiked itself off the floor and – using its stunted roots as tentacle-appendages – scurried off into the forest!

Sleep did not come easily after that.

I don't think Roxana slept a wink.

This morning, I find myself deflated.

How can I ever navigate through a wood, if the trees themselves change places?

I shall continue, but I'm not sure why.

LOG ENTRY: SIXTY-SEVEN Bootprints

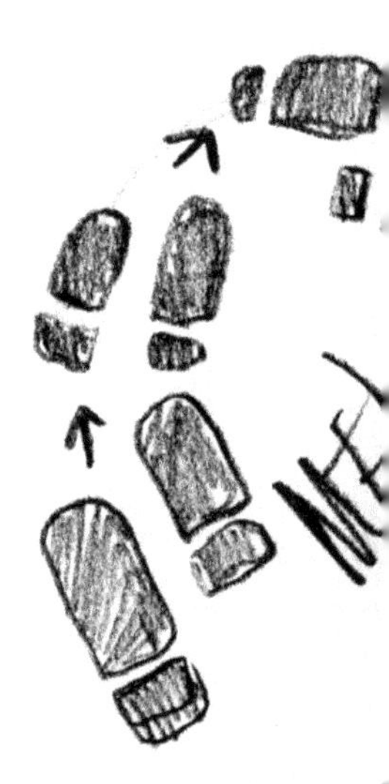

The inevitable has happened.

I have found bootprints in the dirt.

I have been here before.

How long have I been circling myself?

Or worse: squaring?

The bootprints are gone.

Even as I watched them, the ground slowly swallowed them up.

I could have been walking around on the same ground for days.

Weeks?

I am so tired.

Roxana is looking a little worse for wear, too.

For now, I shall sit. I shall see what the evening brings.

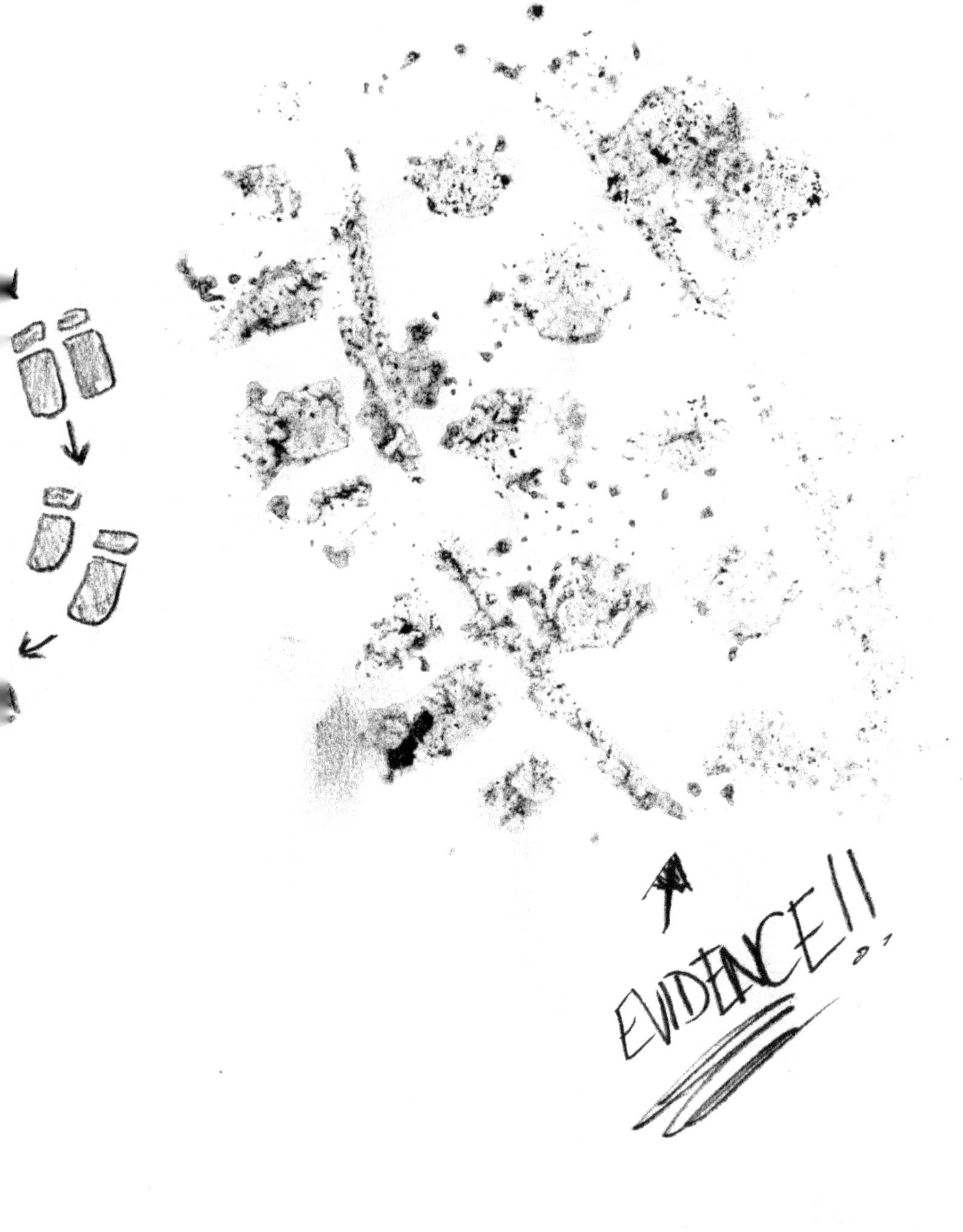

The evening has brought no inspiration.

Just darkness. And loneliness.

Not even Roxana can comfort me.

I am sick of sausage.

LOG ENTRY: SIXTY-EIGHT
New Plan!

BY ALL THE WEATHERED FACES OF THE GUILD,
THAT'S IT!

I'LL TRAVEL BY NIGHT!

AS LONG AS I AM WALKING TOWARDS THE LIGHT,
I'LL FIND THE LIGHTHOUSE!

We leave at once!

(I now realise this is ~~one of~~ the sole
purpose~~s~~ of a lighthouse.
Even so, it is good to have a plan.)

LOG ENTRY: SIXTY-NINE

By Night

CAN SEE LIGHTHOUSE.

MUCH EASIER AT NIGHT.

SAME CANNOT BE SAID FOR SCRIBBLING.

LOG ENTRY: SEVENTY
A Sighting

It is working.

By day, I rest. The landscape is daunting, but I don't think it is dangerous.

By night, I surge onwards – towards the light.

If I ever lose sight of it, I scale one of the more stable-looking trees and seek it out.

It is always there. Guiding me onwards – Like the Flame of the Guild. Only, you know. A lighthouse.

I do not have the strength to scribble any more.

UPDATE!

I have finally caught sight of what Reximus refers to as the lighthouse. It is not a lighthouse like any I have ever seen before.

It is a ship. It is somehow stuck – or suspended – in the cliff face. Some mighty wave must have carried it in from the sea, and deposited it high up along the rocky shore.

There it remains, high above the sea and surprisingly intact. Even so, as far as warnings to other boats go, this is probably about as effective as they come.

It is impossible to tell where the light itself comes from.

Forgive me. I can scribble no more. My strength is failing me and I fear it will be a long, hard climb up to the ship.

But what choice do I have?

NONE! NONE CHOICE!(?)

LOG ENTRY: SEVENTY-ONE
The Climb

I have made it to the cliff.

High above me, the lighthouse throbs.

Come the morn, I shall begin my ascent.

I have prepared the clambering twine.

Roxana is lashed securely to my back.

Wrestler give me strength.

The first part of the ascent is complete.

I shall rest on the rock face tonight.

UPDATE!s

The next part of the ascent is complete!

Woe.

Woe woe woe.

I have made it to the top, but not without great sacrifice.

The last part of the climb was hard. Harder than I could ever have imagined.

The wind picked up and the mist from the sea made every rock sodden and slippery. The salt stung my eyes, blinding me as I groped in the darkness for every handhold.

Then, inevitably, my bleeding hands slipped. I found myself dangling high above the sea by two torn fingers.

No matter how hard I clenched by beard,

I could not pull myself up.

The weight was just too great.

I cannot believe what I am about to enscribble.

I had to

I had to cut Roxana loose.

I could not save us both.

She fell.

It was her or both of us.

HER OR BOTH OF US.

Stumbling and bloody, I made my way to the door of the lighthouse. For some reason, I knocked.

Old habits die hard, I suppose.

Eventually, it opened. With what felt like a deliberately theatrical creak. Some moments later, a wizened old face appeared around it. The face was soon joined by a battered old oil lamp, despite the daylight.

Squinting, the face held its lamp up towards me and a neck extended to crane around the door frame.

"*Whooooooo is it?*" it said in a voice that sounded suspiciously similar to the creaking of the door.

I greeted him with my full list of deeds and titles, as befits a Guildsman. The face listened with impressive patience until I had finished. Then there was a moment of total silence. The face blinked at me.

"*Whoooooo is it?*" it repeated, holding its lamp slightly higher.
"*Codename Alexander McCuba; explorer, bladesman and adventurer of the fabled Guild of Adventures.*" I replied, using the shortest possible rendering of my full title. I extended my forearm in the universal invitation for the clasp of fellowship. The face squinted at my extended (*and bleeding*) hand, then back at my face, then at my tattered feet.

"*And whooooo is this?*" it asked, nodding towards my thigh.
I glanced down. A coconut was dangling from a rope tied around my waist. That was curious.

"*This? This is a coconut...*" I informed the face.

"Why does it have make-up on?"

It was a good question and, for the life of me, I had no idea.

"I believe it is war paint..." I found myself saying. It seemed like a reasonable explanation at the time.

The face's eyes grew wide. *"Is war upon us?"*

"No no..." I tailed off, lamely. We stood in silence for some time. Then, for no discernible reason, the face seemed satisfied.

"Well I suppose you'd both better come in." it muttered and withdrew into the gloom of the lighthouse.

The door closed behind us. It didn't make a sound.

It was her or both of us.

LOG ENTRY: SEVENTY-TWO
The Lighthouse

The lighthouse keeper is called Old Dom, although he can't actually remember how old he is.

My quarters are quite nice.

I left the coconut with the rest of my possessions, in a trunk beside my hammock.

ARCHIBALD!!

He is fine. Thank the Nine Big Faces.

I shall never overlook him again.

ALARM

LOG ENTRY: SEVENTY-THREE GOL

I stayed up late with Old Dom tonight.

We drank a concoction called Gol; it tastes like sweet watery rum, but Dom tells me it is made from fermented cabbage juices from the Glens of Zoosgafistan.

For the good of his health, Dom only breaks it out on special occasions. I asked when he last drank it, but he couldn't remember off the top of his head.

Apparently he was in the process of exporting this Gol (*along with a variety of other cabbage-based produce*) from the Great Port of Quaalpath, when a storm whipped up, blew him many leagues off course and deposited him upon this island. He isn't sure how long ago that was, but he has been here ever since.

Naturally he has tried to leave, but his ship is well and truly stuck in the side of the cliff and the furious waves that pound the shore make escape on a flimsy raft virtually impossible.

After many futile attempts to fend off the waves and get clear of the island, Old Dom eventually resigned himself to manning his ship as a lighthouse to warn others not to come too close.

He isn't sure exactly when that was either, but by the looks of him it was a fair while ago...

I asked him why the ship was called Sweet Yrene.
He didn't answer. I wager he can't remember.

LOG ENTRY: SEVENTY-FOUR
Recovery

I am spending my days with Old Dom sleeping and exercising.

I must recover my strength. I am using a strict routine of Guild Approved exercises techniques, from my Guildsman's Handbook.

Dom is keeping me well fed and in ample supply of things over which I may practise my bounding.

I leaped a barrel of Gol this morning. Dom says I resemble a salmon in flight! I am unsure what to make of this...

Archibald is making use of the time to catch up on his reading. I think.

I wish Sir Charles Biscuit had made it this far.

I think of him often.

SOME GUILD APPROVED EXERCISES :

Beard Raises: grasp an overhanging object (I am using a mast of the lighthouse) and haul yourself upwards until the bottom of your beard reaches your hands. Then lower yourself. Repeat until impossible. The longer your beard, the harder the exercise – but the greater the man.

Guild Squats: slowly drop into a deep squat. Focus your power, then contract all the muscles of the lower body at once, to explosively raise yourself up and off the ground in one fluid motion. Beginners use two legs, intermediates use one leg. Experts use no legs (a very advanced and mysterious technique).

Ground Punch: Lie face down, make a fist and press it into the floor. Focus your power – then punch the ground, to raise yourself up – or push the ground down, depending on your power. Beginners use two arms. Experts end the movement suspended in mid-air.

Beard Sweep: a simple and effective exercise, but one far too difficult to describe here. For the insightful reader: start with your body in a downside-up V position with your hands on the floor in front of you and your backside pointing up to the sky, as a challenge to the Gods. End when you are lying mostly flat on the ground, with your arms raising your head and chest to the sky so you can bellow of your victory. To achieve this involves a diving or swooshing motion, during which you sweep the ground between your hands using your beard.

...etc

LOG ENTRY: SEVENTY-FIVE
Old Dom

Old Dom asked about my family this evening, as we sat on the bridge of the ship looking out over the sea and drinking Gol.
(*It has been exactly one week since I arrived at the lighthouse: this counts as a special occasion.*)

I told him of the Guild: Estoniatus, the Master of Ceremonies, the Guildmaster, Lazy-Face Mary, The Hammer and so on. I recounted our great deeds and even greater feasts, taking extra time over some of my favourite tales. These included the time Hams Sally took a running leap into the Great Lake without realising it had been drained during Quaffer Harris' latest attempt to break the land mead record. The damage to the landscape was catastrophic.

In painstaking detail I described the gargantuan doors of the Guildhall, through which nine burly men can walk abreast without bashing their drinking elbows. Naturally, I went on to describe the laborious task of cleaning and oiling the doors, which usually falls to the apprentices of the Guild, or Guildlings as we call them

Old Dom listened with an expression of awe on his withered/weathered/whether it's even a face. It was either awe or pity; I have been known to confuse the two on many occasions. I ended by explaining my need to escape the island and resume my search for the Great Extravaganza (*whatever that is*).

When I was finished, Old Dom sat in silence for a while, deep in thought.

Eventually, he cleared his throat and started to talk at length about his own family: his wife Yrene and his eleven children, all of whom are named after types of knot:

> Carrick, Cleatus, Buntline, Marly, Transom, Schwasbisch, Rolling Hitch, Slippery Eight, Monkey Fist, Valdotain and, of course, Munter.

Somewhere deep in the folds of his face, Dom's expression lit up when he talked about his children. His eyes twinkled as he recounted Transom's first day of school and, when I asked whether Monkey Fist was a good cook, he roared with laughter and nearly fell off his stool.

"*She couldn't boil an egg if her life depended on it.*" *he guffawed and wiped the tears from his eyes,* "*And of course one day it did...*"
His expression wilted and I tried to change the subject quickly. For some reason, I asked whether Old Dom had any siblings.

He used to have one: a brother called Dom the Younger. He worked the trade routes alongside Old Dom, taking care of the rowing, sailing and navigation whilst Old Dom handled ship maintenance and the vast amounts of paperwork apparently involved in the import and export of cabbage-based produce (*who knew?*).

Dom the Younger was aboard the ship when the storm struck, but by the time the boat was marooned on the islands there was no sign of him. Old Dom has searched the Thundra far and wide, to no avail.

It might be all the Gol, but the beginnings of a plan seem to be forming... Old Dom knows how to build ships, but lacks the man power to do so. I am a powerful man, but I don't know how to build ships. If we combine our skills, we could be in with a shot at leaving this island!

Of course, what we really need is a way of navigating those treacherous waves and finding our way home.

Hmmmm...

DOWN
-THE-

LOG ENTRY: SEVENTY-SIX
A Visitor

I received a visitor today.

He was somewhat soggy, a little battered and absolutely caked in mud, but he seemed in high spirits, from what I could tell.

I had absolutely no idea who or what to expect when I heard the knocking and opened the door to the lighthouse. Even so, I was staggered.

My wheelie board! Don't ask me how it knocked on the door. My mind-reading, self-locomoting, somehow-homing Yewdu Board had managed to hunt me down, still balancing most of my adventuring gear, including my axe, helmet and leather jacket.

Best of all, it brought me my ADVENTURING BOOTS!

Oh, to have them back around my feet again. What bliss!

(They are less comfortable than I remember... I feel I am betraying my entire heritage by admitting that.)

I've seen some pretty remarkable things since I landed on this island, but contraptions made of Yewdu Wood are the most amazing of all.

Now I think about it, I seem to remember Yeti telling me he harvests the wood from this side of the island...

I can feel an idea starting to form somewhere in my beard.

Or a sneeze.

ALARM

LOG ENTRY: SEVENTY-SEVEN

Planning

I'VE GOT IT!

Yeti builds incredible self-locomoting homing boards.

If we throw my board into the sea, perhaps it will carry an SOS message home!

No wait, that's not it.

I'VE GOT IT!

Yeti builds incredible self-locomoting homing boards.

He builds them using wood he chops down in the Thundra using an enchanted axe.

We are in the Thundra.

I have an enchanted axe.

If I chop down some wood and build myself a surfboard, I can ride it home!

No wait, that's still not right.

I'VE GOT IT!

Yeti builds incredible self-locomoting homing boards.

He builds them using wood he chops down in the Thundra using an enchanted axe.

We are in the Thundra.

I have an enchanted axe.

Old Dom knows how to build boats.

If we build a boat out of this Yewdu Wood, perhaps it will be able to sail us safely through the waves and guide us home!

THAT'S IT! THAT'S ACTUALLY IT! FOR ONCE!

IS THIS HOW IT FEELS TO BE FAMOUS?

It's a long shot, but it's the only shot we've got. Apart from shots of Gol, of course, which are reserved for special occasions.

I shall put this plan to Old Dom in the morning.

It was no use. I couldn't sleep a wink: I had to tell Old Dom immediately.

He didn't understand the whole plan to start with, but that's probably because I forgot to wake him up before explaining it. I was very excited.

The second time around, he understood straight away – and agreed!

Tomorrow I shall set out to chop some Yewdu Wood whilst Old Dom starts drawing up some blueprints or...boat-prints...or whatever ship plans are called.

I am still too excited to sleep, so I shall practise my sword forms.

(Lacking a sword, I have had to practise using my axe. It is less versatile, but carries a certain extra heft. I like it.)

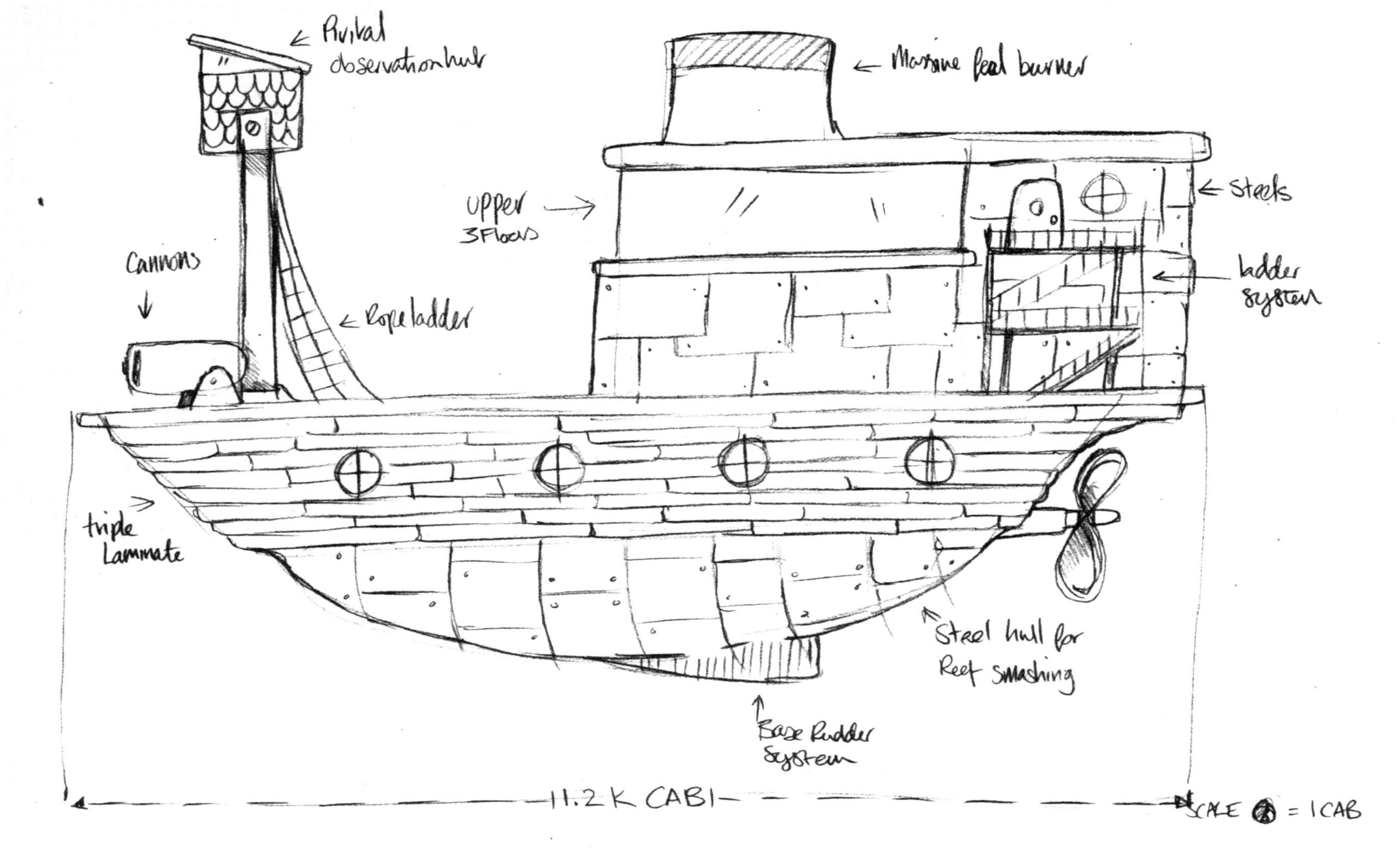

Rivital observation hub
Marxine peat burner
Upper 3Floors
Steels
Cannons
Rope ladder
ladder system
triple Lammate
Steel hull for Reef smashing
Base Rudder System
11.2 K CABI
SCALE = 1CAB

LOG ENTRY: SEVENTY-EIGHT
The Great Wood Choppin'

The wood-chopping is going better than expected. The axe hews through trees as if it was invented for the purpose, which – I only now realise – it was.

Once hacked into plank-like shapes, I load the wood onto my little Yewdu Board – and off we go to the beach, where I unload it, and start over again.

Strangely enough, the trees seem to respond particularly well to being hacked. It is as if they are leaping at the opportunity to make more of themselves. Perhaps I am their Liberator...

This is a serious matter. If I am indeed Liberator of Trees, I will need some...robes, or something. Some symbol of office too, like a sceptre or a large and intimidating ring. I'll probably also have to cut all tree-based produce out of my lifestyle and diet too. I shall miss the bark underpants most.

THINGS I MAY NEED IN CASE I AM LIBERATOR OF TREES

1. A new hat
2. A flag
3. Somewhere to think
4. A thousand-yard stare
5. Some kind of sash or drapery
6. Vision (of the idealistic type)
7. A deep ennui

I wonder what kind of hat a Liberator wears. A fine one, I'll wager. Feathers and buckles. **Brims aplenty!** Perhaps it has a peak, to keep the sun from his eyes whilst he stares deep into the future.

I'll certainly need a note book for all my...inspiring verses. And whatnot.

Alas, such lofty plans will have to wait. We need plenty of planks and this wood isn't going to chop itself.

→ It is not. This I have proved conclusively.

LOG ENTRY: SEVENTY-NINE
Piles o' Wood

Forgive my lack of entries; I have been chopping wood since the dawn of time, or so it feels. Where once were hands, only cramped and blistered paws of uselessness remain. I feel like a potato would feel if it too had spent forever chopping wood.

[That's a bad comparison, I admit. Wood-chopping does strange things to the minds of men. And potatoes.]

Despite the agony, The Great Wood Chopping is complete. All around me are piles – nay...PILES – of wooden planks. It's just as well, too: the Full Moon is just weeks away. Or so I am told. I don't know how Old Dom can tell; there is no discernible pattern to the moon's size or behaviour here.

Even so, I have come to trust Old Dom like the father I never had. I don't trust him quite as much as the father I did have, however. My actual father was the most trustworthy man I ever knew. Until he betrayed us all.

Anyway, considering the fact that we Guildsmen are granted twice our already prestigious strength when the moon is full, it is now imperative that our boat is ready to launch by the time this happens. Only then will we stand our greatest chance of escape.

Let the great ship-building commence!

I shall don the Face of the Smith.

FOR THE GUILD!

SHACKLACKY

LOG ENTRY: EIGHTY The Hull

The framework for our hull is taking shape. It reminds me of the time I saw the colossal skeleton of a flying Yammerfish, one of the primary forms of Zoosgafistanian public transportation. It had been in a mid-air collision with a winged walrus and come off badly.

Come to think of it, I can't imagine what wouldn't come off badly from a mid-air collision with a flying walrus...

THINGS THAT MIGHT SURVIVE A MID-AIR COLLISION WITH A FLYING WALRUS

- A bigger flying walrus
- The Guildhall
- Hams Sally
- Venus (the planet, not the Goddess – she is famously delicate)
- A bronzen water buffalo
- Nine Great Cakes – acting as one Even Greater Cake

I cannot scribble much these days. Every waking moment is taken up with the boat-building process and my hands are still in no fit state for scribbling. Even this short entry has taken an agonisingly long time to craft.

Forgive me. I must stop.

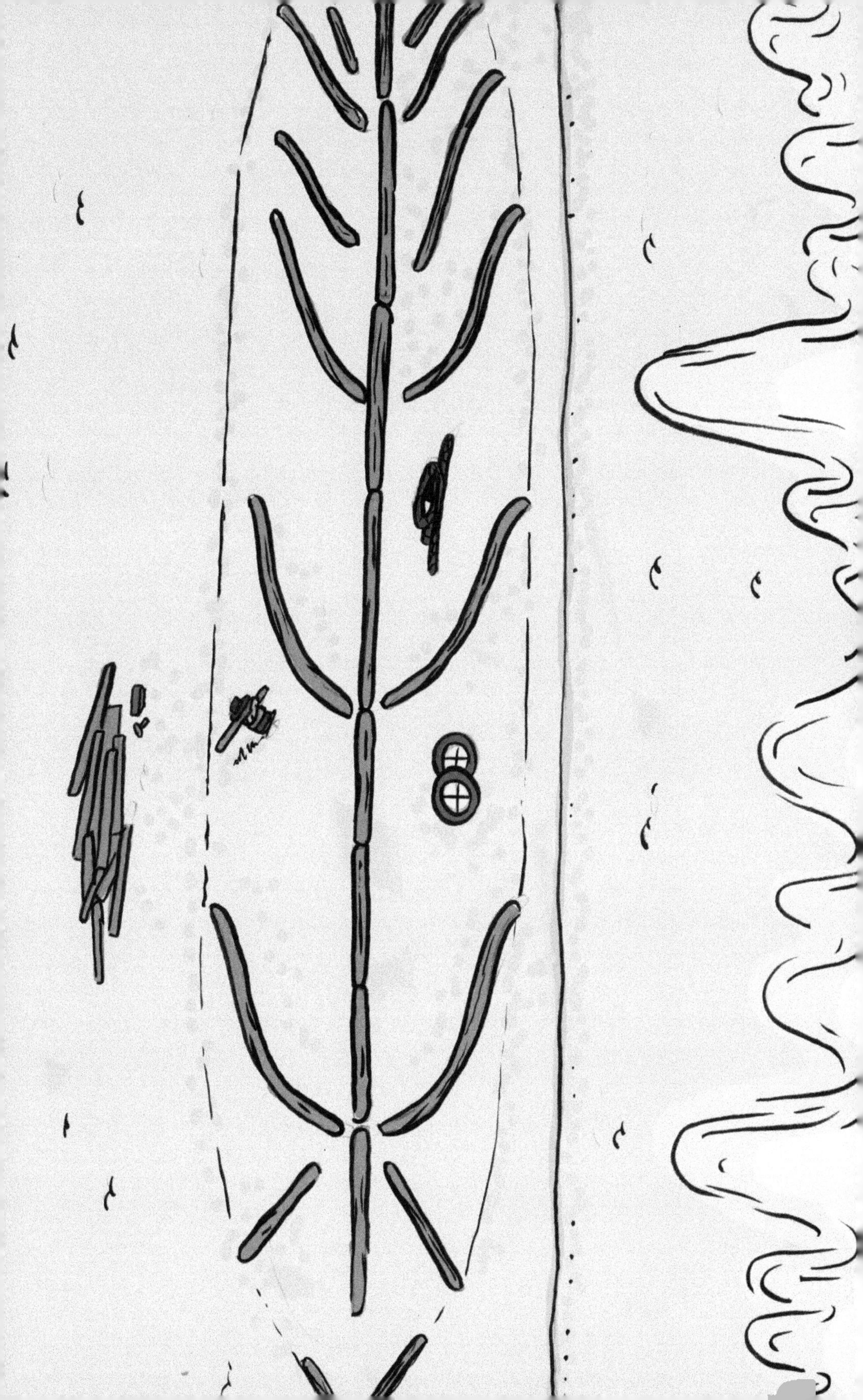

LOG ENTRY: EIGHTY-ONE?
Laminating???

We have started the 'laminating' process, as Old Dom calls it.

Essentially, this involves covering our wooden skeleton in wooden skin. At last, it is starting to look like a boat! Or a sleeping bathtub. I can't really tell the difference, but I suppose that is why Old Dom is leading the ship-building process.

[**IMPORTANT NOTE:** Old Dom gets irritable when I refer to the ship as a "ship". He says it is a "boat". I do not understand the difference.]

Dom says the difference is obvious: "*A ship can carry a boat, but a boat can't carry a ship*". I argue that this isn't obvious at all, and that it also depends on whether the boat is carrying Hams Sally, who can carry anything.

We have settled on the term GuildBoat: *incapable of carrying a ship, but capable of carrying a man who is capable of carrying a ship.*

What we are building, however, is just a boat. Hams Sally might fit into it, but he would render it useless in the process. Like a cow in a bathtub. Or, indeed, Hams Sally in a bathtub.

It is laborious work. Luckily, Old Dom is providing me with a constant source of Gol and other cabbage-based provisions from his vast stores, which are helping me keep my strength up.

OTHER HELPFUL CABBAGE PRODUCTS :

- Soothing cabbage ointment for my blistered hands
- Cooling bandanna made from tangled cabbage leaves dipped in aforementioned ointment
- Sun-toughened cabbage leather gloves for the hefting of planks
- Bite-sized cabbage energy snacks: all the energy of a cabbage in a single chewy mouthful!
- Uniquely fragile ball for relaxing games of Catch t' Cabbage

Who knew the humble cabbage was capable of so much?

Perhaps I shall introduce my fellow Guildsmen to its benefits when I am home. If I dip cabbage in meat sauce, even the Guildmaster might get on-board with the idea...

I doubt it.

SUCH DECEPTION!

LOG ENTRY: EIGHTY-TWO

Today, adrift in a sea of exhaustion, I hammered the final hand-made nail into the hull of our ship and leapt (feebly) for joy.

It was only then that Old Dom informed me that this is merely the FIRST OF THREE layers of laminating required to make the hull truly watertight.

The moon waxes above us. I am so tired. Can we possibly be ready in time?

On the plus side, Dom has come across a rich reserve of unspellable, unpronounceable cabbage beer.

The only way to utter the name of this beer is to attempt to ask for it, then give up at the last moment. The resultant sigh of resignation is the exact correct pronunciation.

I have nick-named it Whine.

I have only just realised how confusing that will become.

I am too tired to come up with a better name.

Whine it is.

LOG ENTRY: EIGHTY-THREE

Finished! (I THINK...)

At long last, we have finished building the hull of our ship. The second layer of laminating took half as long as the first layer and the first three-fifths of the third layer took two-thirds the length of time as the second-half of the second layer.

Don't ask me how I am keeping such accurate records of time. Suffice to say all this cabbage is giving me some fairly tedious super powers, including the ability to accurately judge shades of yellow from fifty paces.

I struggle to tell the difference between Saffron and Golden Rod if I stand on my head after a few bottles of Whine, but I still manage to get it right exactly 72.39554% of the time.

If I say so myself, this hull is a finely crafted thing. No water will be getting through, that's for sure. Although, come to think about it, this seems like the bare minimum one should expect from a boat...

Even so, under Dom's watchful eye and supported by my cabbage-based diet, I have learned much of the art of ship building. Boat building. The Smith would be proud: this hull represents both one of my proudest achievements and a symbol of our imminent departure from this island.

Now we just need to turn it over.

LOG ENTRY: EIGHTY-FOUR

New Drinking Game

I have invented a new drinking game. It is called...

I shall think of a name later. In case I forget, here are the rules:

RULES

1. Pour yourself a cup of Whine
2. Pour yourself a shot of Gol
3. Drink the Whine
4. Immediately drink the Gol
5. Have a lot of fun

It's beautifully simple, like my first wife.

And my second wife, now I think about it.

I shouldn't think about it.

Gol always makes me weepy.

LOG ENTRY: EIGHTY-FIVE Folly

It is no use. Even a man with a back as strong as my own cannot turn this vessel over in the sand. If Hams Sally was here, I expect there would be no issue. Alas, he is not here. Nor are any other Guildsmen. I remain alone.

Apart from Old Dom, of course, but he can barely lift his own head – let alone an entire ~~ship~~. Boat.

Even when this boat is flipped over, there is much left to construct on the other side.

Soon the moon will be full and I shall have twice my strength. Perhaps then I shall succeed in this feat. Of course, I will then have to wait an indefinite period of time for the next Full Moon in order to launch the boat.

So be it. We wait on the moon.

If it is ever completed – which I am starting to doubt – I shall name this boat 'Folly'.

In the meantime...

Gol?

LOG ENTRY: EIGHTY-SIX
Steaks

The failure to turn the boat over has hit me hard. I have gone from being busy from dawn 'til dusk, to having to sit on this beach all day long drinking Whine and staring out at the open sea, dreaming of freedom.
Dreaming of adventure.

To his credit, Old Dom is doing a fine job of trying to cheer me up. Today he even did the dance of his people for me. It wasn't very impressive, but I put that down to Dom's arthritis rather than his people's lack of courage.

For dinner, he found and cooked some fine steaks. It was the first non-cabbage-based meal I have had for quite some time and it was very, very welcome. I do miss barbecued meats.

By the Nine Big Faces...THAT'S IT!

I must return to the barbecue before it runs out...of smoke.

I must summon Reximus!

LOG ENTRY: EIGHTY-SEVEN

Flipping Folly

Reximus arrived this morning, thundering along the beach like...well, like a giant, furry, fire-breathing monstrosity.

He didn't seem impressed that we were intending to leave the island, but he was willing to help us turn the boat over.

In his enormous hands, it was the work of seconds.

We celebrated with sausages and Gol. It was a fine combination and led to extended talks about the possibility of making cabbage-sausages into a realistically marketable product.

Reximus seemed keen. I refrained from pointing out that they would, in all likelihood, have to be steamed.

PROS AND CONS OF CABBAGE SAUSAGES:

Pro

1. Everybody likes sausages
2. The lack of nutritional content will be considered healthy by obese societies
3. ...hmmm.

Con

1. Nobody likes cabbages
2. The lack of flavour will be considered tedious by all societies
3. Cabbages drive you insane

LOG ENTRY: EIGHTY-EIGHT Final Push

Now Folly is the right way up, I have set to work building her ribs and...prongs, and various other elements that Old Dom assures me are necessary for a hard voyage across the open sea.

I have half a mind to tell him that a Guildsman needs nothing more than his meaty palms and the Face of the Oarsman to cover any distance, but it would seem ungracious. I must also remember that Dom is a frail old lighthouse keeper: he will need some creature comforts aboard this vessel, like rum and...something from which to drink the rum.

There is no time to worry about decking, let alone poop decking. We shall live, sleep and navigate from the bottom of the boat like Men of Old. I shall see about affixing some kind of tent of cabbage leather over the top, to keep us dry when the storms inevitably hit.

It is a sign of the times that this does not strike me as odd in any way.

Although we have lost time with the boat-spinning situation, having Reximus around is certainly speeding up the construction process. I do have to keep warning him not to spout flames anywhere near the construction site, however. There have already been a couple of near misses; yesterday **my beard was almost singed!**

I do not want to have to punch Reximus. **Not at all.**

Yet if honour demands it, so it shall be.

Expect very few entries from now on. All haste must be made to finish the task at hand

LOG ENTRY: EIGHTY-NINE

COMPLETE!

It is complete. It being Folly. The boat. Obviously.

We are just in time.

Above us, the Moon is plump and full – like a cabbage. A white cabbage. A...cauliflower?

No, cauliflower is white broccoli. Or is broccoli green cauliflower?

WE MAY NEVER KNOW!

[Note to self: conduct further research into cauliflower/broccoli conundrum. There may be more to this than first meets the balls. Eyeballs.]

The moonshine tingles against my skin. The Guildsman's Tan is a curious thing; I am told we temporarily turn the colour of cold marble beneath the Full Moon's glow. I can feel my strength grow by the minute. It pulses in my beard. With every step I feel my legs urging me to leap, to spin, to kick – to squat the very sky itself!

Colours are clearer. Sounds are crisper. I am aware of everything around me – and every part of myself. When the Moon reaches its very fullest, we shall put our backs to the boat and launch it into the inky midnight sea.

Perhaps we will be able to slip between the waves whilst they are...sleeping?

Then we shall bid farewell to this baffling land of sentient landscapes and overgrown beasties.

I know not what to expect, but I trust Old Dom and I trust our ship. The Nine only know why.

I shall log our sea voyage as diligently as time allows.

LOG ENTRY: NINETY
Cabbages in the Sea

Seventy-nine seconds. That is how long Folly lasted amongst the fearsome Vewdu Waves before she was rent asunder and scattered like apricots in the breeze.

I feel this is an appropriate comparison, but must confess I am not entirely sure what apricots are. I think they are like peaches, but smaller.

I would call such a fruit a Small Peach, but we do not have such things in the Guild. Large peaches, sure – but small peaches? What would be their purpose?

To be frank, I do not believe apricots exist.

I think people have seen juvenile peaches (or peaches that are far away) and confused them for an entirely different fruit. Thus they have created a new name – apricot – for a fruit that already exists and has a name. Peach.

No so for the noble cabbage! Although, now I think about it, sprouts...

By the Nine Faces. Could it BE?!

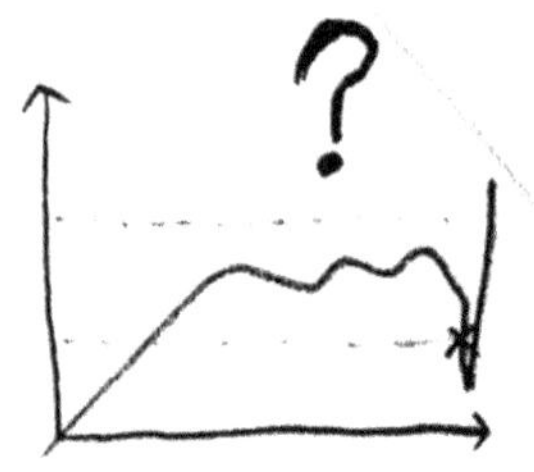

Hold on. I fear I am doing what the Master of Ceremonies would call "repressing" the matter at hand: our boat. Or lack thereof. Much as I appreciate the advantages of most types of pressing (bench, wine and immunosup-, for example), I am sure this is an unhealthy state of mind.

Thus, I confront the issue:

We sped out into the water with the help of a mighty shove from Reximus, who stood on the beach waving a teary farewell. Immediately, it became apparent that Folly couldn't handle the sheer volume of water and verbal abuse. Waves converged on us almost immediately, smashing us between their crests with impossibly agility. My lovingly-hewn woodwork was pulverised like a Small Peach in the battle-callused hands of the Guildmaster.

All the while, the waves hurled insults our way. "Floundering buffoon" was used at one point, as was "Lolloping wearer of pantaloons". Apparently waves enjoy gerunds. I'm not sure why wearing pantaloons is a mockable offence; I suppose that, to a wave, pantaloons must seem rather bizarre.

(*Come to think about it, wearing pantaloons IS rather bizarre...*)

I am almost certain that one of the waves shouted "Nice try, fatso!" as we drifted back to shore. I have convinced myself that it was referring to Old Dom, but I cannot pretend he is anything more than skin and bone these days. Perhaps my cabbage-based diet has en-plumpened my once oaken abdominals.

It seems unlikely, but it has been some time since I have seen a mirror.

Or my toes.

Anyway, our hard work now lies around us in hunks and chunks, little more than pitiful flotsam and uselessly wet kindling. We are not entirely without food because cabbages leaves are buoyant. Who knew?

The whole cabbages themselves, however, sank like...well, cabbages in the sea.

That shall be the name of the poem I shall pen about this incident:
Cabbages in the Sea.

I shall stir fry some leaves for dinner.

Then to bed.

To mope, perchance to despair.

LOG ENTRY: NINETY-ONE
Lights in the Night

I have barely started feeling sorry for myself, yet already another challenge looms.

There are lights. Lights in the night! They have been drawing closer for some time, through the dense trees of the forest.

Please excuse my scribblings: I am having to pen this in the dark, lest the light-bearers spot me.

It was a curious blessing that our wood was too soggy to light a fire this evening.

We remain hidden, but for how long?

UPDATE

The lights have reached the beach. They are blazing torches, held aloft. They may yet pass us by...

Old Dom remains in a deep slumber. Reximus is terrified, bless him.

Archibald is...

Where IS Archibald?!

Wherever he is, he's almost certainly maintaining a stiff upper lip. Stoic to the last.

Oh for the courage of a coconut.

UPDATE

Our discovery is inevitable. I am braced for war. Let the great poets sing of this night: let them emphasise quite how soggy my improvised battle club is.

(Very. It's very soggy.)

FOR THE GUILD

(again)

LOG ENTRY: NINETY-TWO
A Surprise

Sweet relief!

Of all the upon-stumblings I have witnessed, this tops them all!

The battle cry of the Guild had scarcely left my beard when I recognised the first face. Or rather, the first fist. The enormous and unmistakably-glowing knuckles of Metal Ed: they crashed into the side of my head and bowled me over in the sand.

Never have I been so relieved to take a punch.

Luckily, Yeti leapt to my rescue before Ed could continue his assault or Reximus could summon the courage to barbecue the lot of them. As soon as I was back on my feet (*and a few broken teeth had been extracted*), we were leaping around with whatever the manly form of glee is called...

Jubilation?

They were all there! Yeti! Captain Awesome! Metal Ed! Billy Psycho! The entire World Vewdu Wrestling Association was assembled on my beach!

It so happens that this is part of the route for the March of the Vewdu: a voyage into the Thundra that occurs under every Full Moon. That's when Yeti chops the wood for his crafting.

There were others with them too, some I recognised and others I didn't.

"*Dude! We thought we'd lost you!*" Yeti cried, when at last the jubilant jumping had ceased (this took some time).

"*You did!*" I told him. Leaping onto the nearest raised platform (Captain Awesome, as it turned out), I recounted my recent adventures.

The underground passage; the out-spitting; the demise of Sir Charles Biscuit (*may he rest in peace*); the surfboard escape plan; the not-so-slaying of Reximus; my journey to the lighthouse; my time with Old Dom and the folly of Folly – and so on.

I must admit I glossed over the wallowing in self-doubt and embellished the gusto with which I went about my deeds. Guildsman's license, I call it.

The W.V.W.F listened quietly the whole time; such was the drama of my performance. By the end, they only had one question:

"*You're leaving?*"

They seem genuinely disappointed. I am touched. I hadn't really considered that they might enjoy my company.

It is irrelevant now, anyway. Folly is in scraps: I have no choice but to stay.

I suppose it's a good excuse to have a drink!

LOG ENTRY: NINETY-THREE Another Surprise!!

I have just witnessed the most incredible thing.

I poured some Whine for myself and took some to Yeti. We sat looking out over the sea, exactly as we had when I first washed up on these strange shores. Except this time we were in the Thundra; a place Yeti hadn't even wanted to talk about back then.

Yet here he was. Looking for me.

I asked him about Folly. I had been proud of myself for coming up with the plan of using the enchanted axe. I didn't understand what went wrong. Yeti laughed as if I had suggested sitting on the axe and flying it home.

"Dude, there's more to enchanting wood than chopping it with a special axe. Everybody would be doing it if it was that easy!"

Grudgingly, I accepted that he had a point. We sat in silence for a while, then.

"So you really want to leave?" Yeti asked me, eventually.

I told him about my vows to pursue adventure and Old Dom's desires to see his family again. Yeti listened, with a sad but understanding expression on his hairy face. When I had finished talking, he sat very still for a few minutes.

I MIGHT ACTUALLY HAVE A CH

Then he leapt up.

Raising his axe above his head, he began to chant and hop from foot to foot.

In the glow of the full moon, the scattered wreckage of the shop started to sparkle. Then, and this I swear by the Smith's own eyes, it started to reassemble itself! It started slowly, but gradually sped up until the air was ablur with woodwork.

Soon, the rest of the W.V.W.F were joining in, using anything they could find to add bits to our boat until it was barely even recognisable!

Within the hour, a new boat sat shimmering on the moonlit beach.

"*Now THAT is an enchanted ship.*" Metal Ed boomed and clapped me on the back. He had two good points: it was certainly enchanted and, I even checked with Old Dom, it was certainly a ship. It could easily have carried our last boat, with room for Hams Sally and the rest of the Guild too!

Even so, I was still watching the waters suspiciously. The ship was solid (*and magical*) but could it truly survive the pounding of the Yewdu Waves?

Yeti must have guessed what was on my mind because, the next thing I knew, he was waving his hands in the air and three figures were running down the beach.

Gonzo, Bonzo and Alfonzo: the Surfers Three. Tamers of the waves. Boards in hand, they charged into the sea and commenced riding the water.

"*All flaccid*" Yeti said, with a grin.

I must meditate before my voyage.

13

LOG ENTRY: NINETY-FOUR
Yet Another Surprise

What a fool I have been.

All this time I have been worried about escaping this island and resuming my life of adventure, whilst all around me adventures abound! Everywhere I look is a new challenge – something unique to conquer!

→ The Crying Cliff: who will scale his tear-stained face if not the Guildsman?

→ The Roots: who will ride them all and draw up a map if not the Guildsman?

→ The Twisted Peaks: who will climb to their highest point and plant a flag if not the Guildsman?

→ The Thundra: who will trek to its deepest darkest depths and uncover the secrets therein if not the Guildsman?

→ The Voo Brew: who will conduct brutal experiments on his own body in the name of science if not the Guildsman?

→ Who will keep Yeti's shop stocked with Vewdu Wood?
→ Who will endure Captain Awesome's stories from ages past?
→ Who will Metal Ed drink under the breakfeasting table?
→ Who will apply soothing cabbage ointment
→ to Reximus' burned tongue?
→ Who will cut Archibald's hair? (*If we ever find him.*)

Who will journey the length and breadth of this land, until nothing can be seen from the lighthouse that has not been explored?

Who, if not the Guildsman?

FOR LEAVING	FOR STAYING
Continue quest for Great Extravaganza – whatever that is.	Discover more about the Bearhawks
Return to fellow Guildsmen	Fight a Mape
Restock rum	Explore the Thundra
	Document the island properly
	Map the Roots

LOG ENTRY: NINETY-FIVE Farewell

It is decided: I AM STAYING.

Old Dom will leave on his own. Or rather, not on his own – accompanied by a huge supply of Gol and Whine, which he will deliver to the Guild on my account.

The seas are calm and the ship is properly enchanted. Our Vewdu Vessel will see him safely home. Perhaps it will bring him back again someday.

I hope so.

Maybe he will bring the children with him: I would like to experience Slippery Eight's infamously dry sense of the humour for myself.

I shall remain here, to explore these lands and document my findings.

I must also locate my good friend, Archibald.

I have overlooked him for the last time: it will not happen again. Dom has very kindly left me his lighthouse as a base of operations and an ample share of the Whine.

I shall set it up as a Guild Outpost

Perhaps I shall recruit some Guildlings of my own...and teach them to punch. And harvest rumberries. And whatnot.

Glorious times lie ahead.

Guildmaster,

If you are reading this, I trust Old Dom has been successful and that you are enjoying the cabbage drinks.

Please show him your customary hospitality, but spare him some of the more potent rums – his liver is not what it once was.

I have the honour to remain ever-dedicated to the Great Adventure.

Guildsman of the Guild of Adventurers: Longfoot, Jumper of the Jack, The Beef Ranger, Twice Survivor of the Voo Brew, Thrice Winner of the Ham Joust... (The boat is about to depart, so I shall have to abbreviate my list of titles.)

Guided by the Nine Big Faces; sribbled, witnessed and sealed by the light of the Full Moon.

P.S. Send more log books. And rum!!!

P.P.S. I found Archibald.

He was under my hat.

Find out more at : www.deathbyheroism.com & www.happyghetto.co.uk

THANKS, YOU BEAUTIFUL PEOPLE!

Thank you Kerys and Vikki, for listening to us babble, letting this project consume us, and enduring the countless social gatherings that turned into discussing "The Book". Thanks for putting up with our highs and picking us up from our lows.

Thank you Mark, for your creative vision and for pushing us to make this book as epic as possible. We hope we did you proud.

Thank you Ma and Pa Gamester for being a constant source of inspiration and encouragement, and thank you Mum Thorpe for having faith and badgering everyone you know to make this book a reality.

Thank you everybody who pledged on Kickstarter and gave our madness an outlet. We hope you enjoy the result:

Rob Cox
Vikki Moyse
Kev Cook
Tom Allen
Marc Sheinman
Jamie Bennett
Sam Charleston
Michael Pumo
Phill Durham
Christopher George
Doug Jones
Gillain Smith
Jon Cowan
Ingrid Cain
Roger Gash
Peter Toller
Will Ziggy-Stardust
Radha Kanji
Guy Boyle
Thomas Lowe

Matt Bunn
Jitka Hruzova
Will Gamester
Alexandra Jane
Emma Kent
Kaz Bradshaw
William Jones
Victor Beuren
Dan Gates
Carl Snook
Christine Moyse
Steve Gamester
Ade Mills
Emma 'May-k Fist' French
Giles Orford
Chris Brady
Steff Metal
Kenneth Christensen
Lucy Thorpe
Rade Maksimovic
John Gillingham

Gary Clap
Chris Squire
Ryan Vince
Nick Serpant
Pippa Gamester
John Melven
Shelly Noble
Francois got buffed
Kerys Jones
Mark Ruddick
Paul Deegan
Matt Stuttle
Jack Tidy
Garry Sherwin
Dave Hook
Andrew Almond
Petra Eden-Parish
Roy Kamp
Noel Carrigan
Cheryl Daubney